James Milne

The Romance of a Pro-consul

Being the Personal Life and Memoirs of the Right Hon. Sir George Grey

James Milne

The Romance of a Pro-consul
Being the Personal Life and Memoirs of the Right Hon. Sir George Grey

ISBN/EAN: 9783744773331

Printed in Europe, USA, Canada, Australia, Japan

Cover: Foto ©Raphael Reischuk / pixelio.de

More available books at **www.hansebooks.com**

THE ROMANCE OF A PRO-CONSUL

Photo, Russell & Sons, London.

'Sir George Grey's career is a romance'—J. A. FROUDE

THE ROMANCE OF A PRO-CONSUL

BEING THE PERSONAL LIFE AND MEMOIRS OF THE RIGHT HON. SIR GEORGE GREY, K.C.B.

BY

JAMES MILNE

SECOND EDITION

LONDON
CHATTO & WINDUS
1899

PRINTED BY
SPOTTISWOODE AND CO., NEW-STREET SQUARE
LONDON

SUMMARY OF CONTENTS

CONTENTS

vii

CONTENTS

ix

PERSONAL AND PARTICULAR

' PERHAPS there is something in old age that likes to have a young mind clinging to it.'

Sir George Grey was speaking of the famous people he had known in his youth long, long before. He struck an inner note of nature which is surely equally valid the other way ? Whenever I think of the remark, I am inclined to discover one reason why I came to know Sir George so well.

I met him, as I have met other characters of English story in our own day. You go into these great waters, seeking that all who care may know. You cry across them, answer comes back or it does not, and there endeth the lesson, until the next time.

It was different with Sir George Grey. He hauled me straight in-board, saying, ' Now, call upon me often, and we'll talk mankind over. Going by myself, no two people can meet without being a means of instruction to each other, to say nothing else. You are where the swing of events must be felt, and I am in the back-water of retirement. It

B

may entertain us both, to study new subjects under old lights.'

Thus flew many an hour, and many an evening, and the memory of them is green and grateful to me. Here was an incident, there a reflection, and always it was Sir George Grey intimate, whether in a frame large or small. It is the rivulets, babbling to the big stream, that really tell its tale, for without them it would not be ; and so with the river of life. Beside me, a scarred veteran looked back upon himself, hailing some venture from the mist of years. Again, it might be an event on the wing ; or the future, and him bending eagerly forward into its sunshine.

We wrote things, he inspiring, I setting down, and by and by I exclaimed : 'Why, I am getting to be quite a depository of your memories and ideas.' At that he smiled, 'And who, do you fancy, would thank you for them ?' Thus a portrait of Sir George grew with me, and I was for stroking it down somehow. 'Oh well,' quoth he, 'let's try and gather together what may be fresh, or suggestive, in my experiences, and yours be the blame. Whatever you do must have a certain spirit of action—you know what I mean !—or nobody will look at it. You'll need to whisk along.'

In Froude's phrase, the life of Sir George Grey had been a romance, and that was the road which caught me. No wonder, for it was a broad road, in the sense that his whole being was a romance. He saw things beneath a radiant light, and he saw many which to others would have been invisible. Nor, was his grasp of them less accurate, because he strained his eye most earnestly for what was most beautiful. The romantic element in his outlook gave colour, vividness, meaning to the unconsidered trifles—in fine, you had a chronicle and a seer.

On the one hand, then, I sought for the texts with a likely stir in them ; on the other for those of personality, streaked by affairs. The references were consulted, or Sir George's own words of old delved among ; and from his discourse there sprang a regular series of notes. 'It's a kind of task,' he remarked once, 'that might easily enough lend itself to vain-glory. We must avoid that.'

If there is anything that could so be read, I alone am the sinner ; for with his memories there go my interpretation and appreciation of him. What should I do but write of Sir George Grey as I beheld him, of his career as one captured by it ? His nature, like every rich nature, had folds, but I only knew their warmth.

With that, I step round the mountain side.

B 2

HOME IS THE WARRIOR

THINGS call to each other after the great silence has fallen, scenes come together, and that is how it seems here.

A ship, bound on a far voyage, lay in Plymouth waters the day that the Queen succeeded to the throne. It was laden with an expedition for the new wonderland of the Australias, whither it duly sailed. As leader, the expedition had a young lieutenant of the 83rd Foot Regiment, George Grey.

On a spring afternoon, fifty-seven years later, there landed at the same port, from a New Zealand liner, an aged man who received marked attention. He was as a gnarled oak of the wide-ranged British forest, and the younger trees bent in salute to him. It was Sir George Grey, returned finally to the Motherland, which had sent him forth to build nations.

He had gone in a tubby wooden craft, the winds his carrier, across oceans that were pathless, except to the venturer. He returned by steam, through seas which it had tamed to the churn and rumble of the screw. What thought in the contrasting pictures of the world ! The two Englands might have met each other in the street, and passed, strangers.

'From the windows of my hotel at Plymouth,' Sir George recalled, 'I watched the citizens proclaim the young Queen. Who among them could have imagined the glorious reign hers was to be ? It was to surpass in bounty of achievement all foretelling.'

Now, he would meet, for the last time, the Sovereign who, like himself, had tended the rise of Oceana. This was at Windsor, to which he had summons soon after he reached England. He had been exalted a member of the Privy Council, and must be sworn in by the Queen. The tribute was cheerful to him, since the very nature of it set seal upon his services to the Empire. The longing for some word of England's remembrance had assuredly been in his heart, which had often been left desolate. It was all rapture to England, like a child's to its mother.

'For mere honours themselves,' was his broad attitude thereon, 'I entertain no special regard. A title to one's name, a red ribbon, or something else, what are they but baubles, unless there is more ? What more ? Why, they hand down a record of the public work that a person may have endeavoured to perform. In that respect they should have esteem, being the recognition of efforts to serve Queen and people.

'Nothing could be more unfortunate than that a country should neglect services rendered to it. The loss is its own, because, apart from justice to the individual, his example is not kept alive to encourage others coming after. In so far, then, as that reasoning may apply to myself—not very far, perhaps—I do sincerely value any honours I have received. Not otherwise ; and it is easy to understand that a distinction, granted without adequate. cause, might exercise a really pernicious effect upon the tone of a nation.'

While Sir George awaited the Queen's commands at Windsor, she sent him them. He was not to go on his knees, a usual part of the ceremony of swearing in a Privy Councillor. She had remembered, with a woman's feeling, that here was a patriarch, nimble no longer.

The meeting between Queen and servant was stately, in that they were the two people who linked most intimately Great and Greater Britain. To them Oceana was a living, sentient thing, not merely a glorious name and expanse. It had squalled in their ears. They could go back to the beginnings, could witness the whole panorama of the Colonies unroll itself. They stood for the history of a high endeavour, which had been nobly crowned. Oft, there had been weary clouds across the sky, not seldom heavy darkness. But the sun was kept shining, and finally all had become light. Oceana was grown up, and she gathered the four corners of her robe into that Windsor audience chamber.

Of the Queen's order Sir George had the simple deliverance, 'It showed how careful Her Majesty is to manifest a strong consideration for all those who come in contact with her, a most taking quality in a Sovereign.' Yet, for the first time in his life, he was to disobey that Sovereign. Nothing, not even her protest of 'No, no,' could stop him from getting down on his knees, as if he had been a younger subject. The infirmities were conquered by his desire to pay to the Queen that reverence and loyalty which had always been hers. The bonds of age were burst, although his quaint complaint about himself that very evening was, ' You know I want a minute or two to get in motion.'

Despite bowed shoulders and rusty joints, he still had something of the lithe, strenuous carriage of his youth. In his dignity of manner, there almost seemed to you a glimpse of the gallant age when forbears had gone whistling to the headsman. He was of a line which counted in English history, which among its women had a Lady Jane Grey. His mother, with the mother's wistful love and pride, had traced that line for him. He was not deeply moved, unless by the romance and the tragedy that gathered about it.

But the aristocrat abode in the democrat, nature's doing. He was of the people in being whole-souled for them ; he was not by them. Verily, he had been through the winters in their interest. The ripe harvest was in his hair, which had become thin above a face, rugged with intellect ; over a broad, decisive brow, strewn with furrows. It was a head of uncommon shape, with bumps and a poise, indicating at once the idealist and the man of action. There it spoke truly, for Sir George was both ; the two were one in him.

The chief secret of his personality seemed to rest in his eyes, and it was in them you met the dreamer of dreams. ' So I was often called,' he would mention, ' and the answer is to hand. Many of the dreams which I dreamt have been realised ; that knowledge has been permitted me. Whether it is any comfort I'm not sure, because, after all, my dreams are not nearly exhausted.

' Dreaming dreams ! I trust that Englishmen will never cease to do that, for otherwise we should be falling away from ourselves. To dream is to have faith, and faith is strength, whether in the individual or in the nation. Sentiment ! Yes, only sentiment must remain, probably, the greatest of human forces governing the world.'

The store, reflected in Sir George's eyes, was what gave him his control over men. In those depths, blue as a summer sky, were many lights, which caught Robert Louis Stevenson and were comprehended of him. The return observation was, ' I never met anybody with such a bright, at moments almost weird, genius-gifted eye, as that of Stevenson.' Sir George could fire imagination in the most ordinary mortal, carrying him off into enchanted realms. He sailed to strange skies, a knight-errant of a star, and he could tow the masses with him. He lifted them

8

out of themselves, and put a label on their vague
yearnings. They had imagination, the instinct upward, and were grateful to have it discovered.

The poetry of Sir George's nature flavoured his
language, alike in manner of delivery and turn of
phrase. It had a quaint old-world style ; it fell
slowly, in a low, soothing voice. He might have
spent his days in the cloister, rather than in the din of
hammering up hearths for the Anglo-Saxon. Perhaps
it was that he had talked so long to the hills of
Oceana, catching their simplicity and music. You
were reminded of the measured English of an old and
lovable book, just as you grew used to read in his
face what he was to say, before the words had begun
to flow. Never was there a face more quick to
reflect the mind, more pliable to humour, more
luminous at some stirring idea or deed, more indignant
at the bare notion of a wrong inflicted, softer at the
call of sympathy.

Sir George had travelled to Windsor with the
Earl of Rosebery, then Prime Minister, and that was
an agreeable memory. Being asked what characteristics he noted as most prominent in the Premier, he
replied : 'Oh, his extraordinary readiness at seeing the
humorous side of anything, his almost boyish love of
fun. He seems to have a power of dismissing the
weight of public affairs, of diverting himself with the
playfulness of youth.' Sir George was living in Park
Place, St. James's, and on returning from Windsor
the Premier drove him there. His rooms were at

Number 7, and here the street ended in a sharp incline, with somebody's yard beyond.

Sir George suggested that the coachman should stop, and let him down at a point where the horses could readily turn. 'Not at all,' Lord Rosebery insisted, 'I'll drive you to the door and we'll manage to turn somehow.' A trifle anxious, Sir George waited on his doorstep to see how this was to be done.

'Quick of eye,' he related, 'the coachman discerned the possibilities of the yard at the top of the incline. Accordingly, he whipped into it, wheeled round, and trotted gently away past me. There sat the Premier in the carriage, waving his hat in a triumph, the fun of which quite infected me.'

Sir George appreciated kindly attentions the more, in that he was himself a king in courtesy, with his heart ever on the latch. He estimated the side of Lord Rosebery's character, thus manifested, to be among the best ornaments he could have. 'It seems clear to me,' were his words, 'that he is a man of sincerity and simple nobility, one who wishes with all his heart to do what he can for his fellow men.' That was Sir George's test of all public effort, as it had been what he applied to himself. There could be none higher.

Mere weight of years, could not quench the ardour and hope which had always burned so brightly in Sir George Grey. As well expect him to forget that chivalrous manner of his, bewitcher of the veriest stranger. He would find his tall hat, search out his staunch umbrella, and convoy the visitor forth, when the hour of parting had arrived. Nothing less would suffice him, and as to his company, it was a delight for ever. Another veteran might have been lonely with a younger generation knocking at the door, indeed in full possession. He was not ; he strode in the van with the youngest.

Yet he felt, perhaps, the void time had wrought in the circle of his friends. He held the fort silently, while the long scythe cut another swathe very near him. He heard that his friend, James Anthony Froude, who had been lying ill in Devonshire, was steadily losing strength.

'I have made inquiries about him, poor fellow,' he murmured, 'but now I must telegraph for the latest particulars. He and I are old companions, and I have liking and admiration for him. When he visited me at my island of Kawau, off the New Zealand coast, we had a capital while together. He wanted to ask me, if I approved the manner in which he had written Carlyle's life, a subject that brought him a good deal of criticism. My reply was that I believed Carlyle would have wished to be presented just as he was ; not a half picture, but complete, for that would ultimately make him appear all the greater.'

Somewhat before his illness, Froude published a book, and the London daily paper which Sir George Grey took in, had a handsome review of it. 'I'll send the cutting to Froude,' he declared ; 'it will do him good to know that his latest writings are thoroughly appreciated.' Within a few days, he had news from Devonshire that Froude had been able to have part of the article read to him, and that he was gratified by it. Sir George was happy at his little service having carried so well, and mentioned a larger one which Froude had wished to render him.

'Hardly was I in England this time,' the history of it ran, 'than I had a letter from Froude, intimating how glad he would be to put my name forward for that high distinction, the Oxford honorary degree. This gave me a grand chance to rally him, since I was already in possession of the honours of Oxford and Cambridge. Those of the former I received after my first administration of New Zealand, those of the latter when I was re-called from South Africa. At Oxford, the students, with riotous zest, sang the "King of the Cannibal Isles," which, more or less, I had been. Froude had forgotten all that, but he agreed that no man could hope to have such a treat twice in a lifetime.'

It would have been curious if Sir George, a maker of British Parliaments, had not found his way to their cradle at Westminster. He had himself been a candidate for membership, but the House of Commons was only to know him as a visitor. 'Why,' he said, 'I met Adderley, now in the Lords, who once wanted to impeach me. Perhaps I deserved to be impeached—I don't remember !—but anyhow we had a very agreeable chat about old days.' Sir George, as a

Privy Councillor, had been escorted to the steps of the throne in the House of Lords. There he met again the Marquis of Salisbury, who, as Lord Robert Cecil, had stood up for him, years and years before, in the Commons, even to the extent of criticising the English of Bulwer Lytton's despatches. When he went to Australasia, to fortify his health and study the New World, he was the guest, for a period, of Sir George in New Zealand.

'Some of his friends,' said the latter, 'were great friends of mine; for example, Beresford Hope, who founded the "Saturday Review," and Cook, who edited it. Lord Robert was tall and slight, and, when he came to New Zealand, not at all strong. While he was with me, he saw a good deal of the manner in which a Colony was conducted, and of the relationships between it and the Mother Country. He would read the despatches that I wrote and received, and generally made a study which may have proved useful to him in his subsequent career.

'As I recollect Lord Robert Cecil in New Zealand, he was not more fond of exercise than Lord Salisbury appears to be to-day, always being studious. He did not care to take long walks, but once I persuaded him, with another young Englishman, to go and see the beautiful Wairarapa Valley. They walked there and back, and on the last evening, while returning, were caught in a terrific rain-storm. They sought the shelter of some rocks, contrived to make a fire, and over it dried their shirts.'

Nothing afforded Sir George more genial occupation than a talk about books or politics, the latter always on the lofty ground to which, somehow, he could at once lift them. He had a knack of taking a question and shaking it on to your lap. You had it, as you never quite had it before, and to your fascinated ear the version seemed the only possible one. The secret was that Sir George laid hold of the kernel of a subject, and worked outwards—an expositor, not a controversialist. When evening waned he would turn to Epictetus, and then to a well-thumbed New Testament. It was the hour of meditation.

'I have studied the New Testament in various languages,' he said, ' thus getting more insight of it than I could have got through a single language. Never, during my early exploring work, was I without my New Testament to comfort and sustain me. The Sermon on the Mount is the great charter of mankind, its teachings the highest wisdom for all times and all climes. It and other pieces, which I might select, are of exceeding beauty and full of guidance and counsel. They inculcate in the human heart a love of one's fellows, irrespective of colour.'

He read that teaching into the happier London which greeted him, after an absence of more than twenty-five years. At last, the museums and art galleries were really open to the people, who thronged them, drinking in knowledge. He noted the children playing in the parks, and they were better dressed, the parks themselves better kept. You can judge a nation by the state of its children's boots, and these had fewer holes. The poor London had, and ever would have, but she was not the callous mother of other years. She felt for those who were down.

Sir George would ride by 'bus, except, indeed, when in pursuit of some volume for that beloved library at Auckland. Then, nothing would satisfy his eagerness but hot foot and back with the trophy, scanning its pages in his scholar's joy. But a-top the 'bus was the working man, homeward bound, and he was getting more out of life. Manhood was in him, he evidently had at last a free, firm seat in the saddle of which Providence had always held the stirrup.

The feeling of human brotherhood was wider, deeper, the benefits springing therefrom apparent all round. Penny fares were bringing classes into contact with each other, who were formerly as far divided as if they had lived in different planets. The London policeman's upheld hand, was an eloquent speech on the sacred meaning of law to a free people. Youth helped age to a seat in a public vehicle, and the brick-layer quenched the fire of his pipe because the smoke annoyed a lady sitting behind him.

Sir George would have built a bricklayer's statue on the best site that London could provide. Not that he was fond of statues, unless they happened likewise to be art ; but that such a one would have carried its meaning. There was already a statue of himself at Cape Town, and his Auckland admirers had a scheme for another.

'No doubt they'll take care it does you justice,' he was joked.

'Well, I don't know,' he answered, a smile puckering his face, 'but perhaps they should wait until I'm gone. They might want to pull it down again, if I did not behave all right. Now, that would hurt my feelings.'

III

YOUTH THE BIOGRAPHER

ONE to whom the beyond is near, who has the kindled vision, probably best sees the life he has lived, in the beginnings—child, boy, and youth. There are no smudges on that mirror.

The stage of being which we call childhood had an endless charm for Sir George Grey, and often that drew him back to his own early years. The little child, a bundle of prattling innocence, still on the banks of the world's highway, like a daisy nodding into the flying stream, was in his sight almost a divinity. Here was the most beautiful, the most perfect manifestation of the Creator ; an atmosphere where the wisest felt themselves the babes.

'You are the one Englishman living,' Olive Schreiner, when in England, wrote to Sir George before calling upon him, 'of whom I should like to say that I had shaken his hand.'

But it would not, she continued, be the first time they had met, for, during his rule of Cape Colony, he had visited the mission station where her parents dwelt. She thought this was while Prince Alfred was on his tour in South Africa; anyhow, when she was an infant, a few months old, ailing, hardly expected to live. The Governor took her in his arms, saying, as her mother related to her, ' Poor little baby ! is it so ill ? '

'When the other children teased me,'—Olive Schreiner had her triumph from the incident—' I could say to them, " Ah, but you were not held in the arms of Sir George Grey ; " and that was safe to bring about an increased respect on their part towards me.'

Taking his walks in Kensington Gardens, Sir George would make friendships among the small people whose nursery coaches are there the swell of a thoroughfare. On the second occasion of meeting he might be expected, with a fine show of mystery, to produce a toy from his pocket. ' It's so easy,' he remarked, ' to convert these gardens into a fairy-land for some child whose name you only know because the nurse told it you.' Then, a favourite would not be met one day, or the next, and Sir George would feel a blank in his walk.

At his own fireside, a girlie with rosy, dimpled cheeks, straightway made him her subject, by the simple trust with which she took his outstretched hand, cuddled on to his knee, and sat enthroned. She confirmed a victory, that he regarded as all his, in a most faithful treatment of tea-cakes, protesting at every mouthful, ' Oh, no, I sha'n't be ill ; I *won't* be ill ! '

It had been the same when Sir George was among
the Aborigines of Australia, for the children promptly
made friends with him.   The grown natives, never
having seen a white before, had sense to be scared.
Their bairns merely had intuition, and it took them
to Sir George's side, which, again, brought in the
parents.

Studying a portrait of his own father he mused:
'The child that has never known both parents, must
be conscious of having missed part of its inheritance
in the world.'   He had been thus robbed, a few days
before his birth, by the slaughter at Badajoz, where
Colonel Grey fell, a gallant soldier, scarce past
thirty.

To a problem which the youngest child carries
lightly, Sir George had given much thought, namely,
'Of what does human life consist? what are its
elements?'   Thereon he had the deliverance:

'Quite early in my own life, I formed the opinion
that we had neglected to consider an element of existence; that besides the solids and the fluids there was
ether. It seemed to me that ether played a very important part, alike in the creation and the maintenance
of life.   That was the everlasting ingredient, the
something which never perished, but went on and
on, the soul in the body of flesh and blood.   Brought
into contact with various eminent men, I was happily
able to discuss such vital questions with them.'

Sir George's mother first set him thinking, and
he had a recollection of learning the Lord's Prayer

from her. Indeed, his earliest mental problem arose from the opening words, 'Our Father, which art in Heaven.'

'I took the "which art in" to be all one word, and puzzled over its possible meaning. The circumstance was a light to the obstacles that beset a child's mind, and a lamp to parents in training that mind. Never was there a mother more fitted than mine, for the glorious responsibilities of motherhood. Very highly educated, she added Latin to her other accomplishments, in order that she might teach the language to me. She had married a second time, and my stepfather, a wise and large-hearted man, one of the best men I have ever known, also bestowed much care on my upbringing.'

As a little fellow he had lived a good deal in London with relations, a family of whom had a house near Hyde Park. He could call up, from the farthest caverns of his memory, a Sunday forenoon on which he was carried off to church, because there was nobody at home, except the servants, to look after him.

'What West End church it may have been I cannot tell,' Sir George said, 'but I imagine the one the household usually attended. The other detail that a fire burned in our pew, did impress itself definitely upon my mind. I was at least big enough to lift a poker, and what must I do but seize that instrument, and set to scraping the fire, to the confusion of those with me. Perhaps the idea of a fire in a church pew may be deemed curious at this date, so much later. But why not? It was really a great boon to those worshippers whom delicacy of health might otherwise have kept at home. For, of course, there was then no better means of warming a church.

'The house of another London relative was in Lombard Street, looking on to Old Change Alley, and there, likewise, I was a pet. A store of books filled one of the rooms, and it was my delight, having already learned to read, to pick out diverting volumes. There were accounts of the travels of Captain Cook and other explorers, and these quite caught my fancy. I felt I should like to travel, when I grew up, and this glimmering idea was advanced by the contemplation of a fruit stall that did business in Change Alley. I marvelled from whence came the oranges and bananas, and I whispered to myself, "I'll go where they grow." '

Some afternoon, Sir George journeyed down to Lombard Street, in order to revisit his ancient shrine. He returned triumphant with the news, 'Would you believe it? I have found many of those old books just where they were, so very long ago. Dear me! the discovery almost took my breath away, and a sort of lump was in my throat.' And the orange stall? Aye, even it lingered; at least there was still a stall in Change Alley. London had not rolled over it.

The romance of war descended to Sir George Grey on his mother's side, as well as from his father. She was daughter to a military officer, whose exploit at the siege of Gibraltar she recited to her boy. It was that of a derring-do soldier.

He happened to be on leave, from his duties at the fortress, when the famous siege began. He hurried to the neighbourhood, laid hold of a boat, and actually rowed through the Spanish fleet. The British garrison gave him a tremendous reception, and the officers marked his feat by the gift of a gold snuff-box. He was thrice welcome : for himself, for the coolness with which he had broken the blockade, and for the news he brought from the outside.

The precious snuff-box descended to Sir George Grey, an heirloom that suggested an adventure of his own. He was sent to a school at Guildford in Surrey, and he ran away from it. He found the teaching all towards the classics, making for Oxford or Cambridge, and afterwards for a learned profession. His real nature, as modelled chiefly by his mother, was in the direction of public service, with, he hoped, some stir in it. The escape from the school he always related, as if the pages of Robert Louis Stevenson were open in his hand at the flight of Alan Breck among the heather.

'I was determined to get home and tell my folks what I wanted to do. Moreover, the walled playgrounds, the being shut in from nature, the walking in line at exercise—these things were insupportable to me. It was like keeping a boy's spirit and imagination in prison, instead of allowing them free communion with the world around. Farther, I was angry at boys having been put over me, for their knowledge of classics, who were perfectly ignorant of the higher branches of knowledge at which I had been working. "Clever but idle" was usually the character I got at school. They didn't understand me, for I studied one subject while they wanted to test me by others.

'Well, accompanied by a boy friend, I climbed over the wall of the school at Guildford, and made for home. My step-father's place was at Bodiam, about twelve miles from Hastings, and between Bodiam and my London relatives I had lived before going to Guildford. But at this time, if my memory does not mislead me, the family were at Eastbourne. In that case my destination would have been Eastbourne, and I know the route taken was by Brighton. We had left as darkness was falling, and I'm afraid we hadn't much money for the journey. That scarcely mattered, however, since we were walking, therefore having no outlay unless for food. We slept a night under the cliffs at Brighton, and I don't doubt we slept very soundly. Boys do, anywhere. People were kind to us, and when asked, we made no secret of the fact that we were fleeing from school.

'It had been arranged, between my companion and myself, that I should take him into our house. At Eastbourne, which we reached sorely tired, our insurgent spirits somewhat calmed, we had quite a lively reception. There appeared to be, on the part of the younger members of the family, a fear lest we should be instantly executed. Nothing so dreadful happened. The other boy was put into communication with his friends, and I had a long holiday. By and by, under the charge of a friend, I returned to Guildford to make explanation and excuse. That done, I went visiting more relations at Cheltenham— I had a lot altogether, you see !—and there I was brought under the influence of Whately, later the renowned Archbishop of Dublin.'

The boyish spirit kept alive in Sir George, and in that respect he had a surpassing encounter. He spent holiday hours in the Natural History Museum at South Kensington, near which he resided after leaving St. James's. There was hardly an animal, or bird, that he could not instruct you upon ; but his delight was to watch the streams of happy visitors. As he sat thus of an afternoon, half a dozen boys gathered round a specimen from animal-land placed near by.

Boys have few doubts, but these lads had theirs as to the identity of the beast. They noticed Sir George, and a delegate approached him with the request, ' Please, sir, can you tell us the name of this creature ? '

He turned in the direction indicated, and found, strangely enough, that the specimen was one which he had sent home from the far south, during his naturalist's work there. He named it, and the lad followed up, ' Where did it come from ? ' ; getting the answer.

Next, ' Who killed it ? ' A pucker gathered upon Sir George's face, and he hesitated, arguing with himself, 'If I tell them, they'll think me an impostor, and even discount the information I have given them.'

But the inquisitor waited, and Sir George could do no better than 'Frankly, you know, I believe, I killed it myself.'

'Here, you fellows!' the merry voice rang out; 'he says *he* killed the beast! Did you ever?'

The other boys left the animal to stare at what they felt to be a greater curiosity.

'Oh, yes,' Sir George addressed them, as they formed a half-circle before him, 'what I have told you is quite true. But if you will listen, I'll relate the whole story, and then you can decide for yourselves.'

He began the tale, the amused incredulity of the boys quickly vanished, and he never had a more attentive audience. When he had finished, his auditors raised their hats and caps with a hearty and convinced 'Thank you, sir.'

He gravely saluted them, as was his custom towards young and old, high and low, and then he fell a-dreaming. He was out walking in the pleasant English woods with Whately, learning from him the manner in which the ancient Britons lived, and how they dug for pig-nuts; or Whately rubbed dry sticks against each other, the primeval manner of making fire. More, he concentrated, with a glass, the rays of the sun upon a handful of dry twigs, which at the bidding went ablaze. Still another picture!

' While I was at Cheltenham, Whately was court-
ing a connexion of mine, who later became his wife.
She put me through my tasks, and Whately would
help her in that, I sitting between them. Did
ever a boy at his lessons occupy a seat of such
influence ? I suppose I could have commanded my
own terms in reference to them, and perhaps I did.
They were most pleasant for all concerned. My education altogether, as a boy, was not very systematic, but
it was broad and useful.'

Finally to Sandhurst, where Sir George did so well
that the authorities had quite a special word for him ;
and where one of the teachers, a Scotsman, gave him
Bacon to read.

With his military studies he combined others,
working even to elucidate the Surrey remains of the
Romans, whose glamour as rulers hit him.

IV

SAXON AND CELT

IRELAND, which has sent so many of her own sons across the sea, was to exercise a real influence upon the going of Sir George Grey.

He was, perhaps, in a special degree, kindly of thought and act towards Irishmen, fancying that as a race they had suffered, and liking their humour, buoyant against all odds. Several Irish political prisoners were released, after serving long sentences, and Sir George read an account, given by one of them, of the gaol experiences. Herein, complaint was made of the distress caused by the flash-flash of the turnkey's lantern, into the cells, all through the night. He went his rounds, and as he came to a cell door he flared his lantern inward by its little opening, making sure of the inmate. It was to the mind and nerves, what a red-hot wire would have been, driven into the body.

Next morning Sir George said, ' I could not sleep for thinking of that light, jab-jabbing the poor fellow in his cell. Nay, it appeared to be in my own bed-room, searching for my face and challenging me, " Are you there ? Ha, ha, are you there ?" What an eerie torture, to a slumbering soul, in that recurrent flame from the prison darkness ! The thing stings and shocks me.'

It gnawed. His heart was full, and perhaps also his mind with the idea, 'Is it ours to impale the soul as well as the body of a fellow-creature ? Surely that is reserved for a higher tribunal !'

The up-come of Ireland would provoke a story affecting Sir George Grey in a family sense. An ancestor, Ram by name, of his step-father had figured in a somewhat sudden meeting with Dean Swift. This was Sir George's telling of it :

'Dean Swift, in a modest phaeton, happened to be jogging past Gorey, the residence of Ram. At that moment, out of the gate drove the more imposing carriage of the latter, and there was a collision. The Dean and his phaeton were thrown into the ditch, but neither, by good luck, suffered hurt. Instead of uttering words, which even the cloth might not have suppressed in some, the witty Dean shot these lines at Ram's apologetic confusion :

> Here's Ireland's pride and England's glory
> Upset by the great Ram of Gorey.

The Ireland, to which Sir George's military duties introduced him, might have driven laughter from all but Irishmen. Turmoil and discontent gripped the land; naked want was among the people.

The green island smiled winsomely in the Atlantic,

only to belie itself as an abode of happiness. Its plaintive atmosphere wisped round Sir George Grey, as a mist enwraps two walkers on a Scottish hill-side, sending them silent. He was young, sensitive, sympathetic, and environment moulded him, as already it had done in the larger island, also with its suffering masses. Sir George had extracts of memory which afforded a vivid idea of Ireland in the early Thirties.

'I was'—he picked out this incident—'a guest at a dinner where I heard the toast " The Protestant King and confusion to Roman Catholicism." Just reflect on what that meant ! Think of the injustice, the intolerance, the lack of ordinary human feeling thus put into a sentiment ! A Roman Catholic gentleman was present, and, knowing what was coming, he good-naturedly rose and left the room, observing that he would join the ladies. Yes, that was an Irish gentleman !

' Again, my heart was wrung at what I witnessed, while in command of a party of soldiers, under orders to protect a tithe-collecting expedition. To me it appeared wrong, shameful, un-Christian, that money for a Church which preached the love of God and His Son towards mankind, should be wrung from the people by armed soldiers. More, it seemed to me nothing less than blasphemy, a mockery of all true religion, and I thought it terrible to have to bear a part in the business.'

Yet, as ever among Celts, these shadows had edges of the lightsome. The tithe-gatherers would be out to distrain in a particular parish, and find loads of the humble chattels, which they meant to seize, already carted over the boundary into the next parish. That, Sir George explained, was a familiar trick to play upon the tithe-gatherer, who could not budge beyond the phrasing of his warrant. It was a beating of the parish bounds, such as he could not always be prepared for. The peasants would stand in sanctuary, with quick, mocking tongues, pointing the finger of scorn. It was trying work for the soldiers of the people, since they had to forget that relationship.

On such an affair Sir George, then a subaltern, made a report to his commanding officer, and it went wider than routine. He offered a frank account of the events attending the tithe-collecting, including the attitude of the peasantry, and the lessons that occurred to himself. These, the commanding officer did not desire, and he returned the report to the writer, desiring it to be made formal. 'Sir,' was the subaltern's reply, 'I have stated just what happened, and I should wish, with your permission, to abide by my report.' He awaited results with a mixed interest, but the farther history of that temerarious despatch he never learned. It may, or may not, have reached all concerned.

Of the Irish race Sir George conceived the warmest opinion, holding them to be the owners of many virtues. Especially they were brotherly of nature, truly generous of heart, and chivalrous of action. He had one proof of the last quality in a curious-falling in with some Mayo smugglers. What better evidence of the innate chivalry of a race, than to find them instinctively expect it in a stranger ?

'There were,' he narrated, 'very stringent regulations in Ireland, in regard to the illicit distilling of spirits. It was another disagreeable duty for soldiers that they had to accompany revenue officers in the search for stills. Now, I was very fond of shooting, and when the opportunity arose I would start off with my gun. The country folk might always be applied to for information as to the spots most likely to furnish a shot. They were perfect hosts to the Saxon as an individual, though otherwise to the Saxon engine of government.

'Being abroad one day with my gun, I noticed a group of peasants at work in a field. Anxious for their counsel towards a bag, I jumped the wall into the field where they were. What was my astonishment to discover that I was in the midst of an illicit still ! You can imagine my position ! I, an officer holding the King's commission, had, as a private person, become aware of an offence against the law. My worry was so keen, over the awkward relationship in which I stood towards the party, that I expressed it.

'"It is," I said, "frequently my duty to protect preventive men, and if that duty were ever to bring me this way, you would feel that I had informed upon you." "No, no," was the answer in chorus, "you only protect the excise men, that forming part of your duty; you are not an informer but a protector, and we know you won't tell." They were good enough to emphasise this vote of confidence with an invitation that I should try their poteen. Naturally I declined, but in a manner, I hope, calculated not to wound their feelings.'

This demeanour Sir George Grey carried into his office as a centurion of soldiers, at a date when the lash still plied viciously in the British army. He sat on a court-martial which had to try a private soldier for habitual drunkenness. As the youngest officer present, he was the first to be asked what the sentence ought to be. He suggested a light punishment, one that was not perhaps in harmony with ideas then prevalent as to the best manner of preserving military discipline. To him flogging was abhorrent, and entertaining that view, he had fallen into debate with brother officers. The sentence which he proposed caused a roar of laughter among some of the members of the court-martial. 'Gentlemen,' interjected the general at the head of the table, 'mercy is a very becoming characteristic of youth, and I do not understand this laughter.' That cut it short.

Daniel O'Connell was at the height of his influence in Ireland, and Sir George could look back on the military duties which once or twice brought him into the precincts of the Tribune.

'Agitate, agitate, agitate,' a sympathetic Viceroy had written to O'Connell, upon the subject of Catholic emancipation, and an official stir followed. The

Marquis of Anglesey, who led the cavalry at Waterloo, and lost a leg there, had not hesitated to utter his mind about Ireland. O'Connell unthinkingly read the letter at a meeting, and the Viceroy found himself in trouble with his Government. That was within Sir George's memory; but take, as touching O'Connell more intimately, an election meeting at Limerick, where the regiment was paraded to keep order.

'With a bitter satire, O'Connell introduced into his speech,' said Sir George, 'the story of the siege of Limerick. He eloquently told how the women of Limerick beat back the soldiers of William III. This was his shrewd method of getting at us soldiers, and he implied that, if necessary, the women of Limerick could beat back the soldiers of another English king. All we could do was to stand there, stiff as starch, while the stings fell from his caustic tongue. O'Connell was a splendid speaker, and he had a most inviting presence, an attractive personality altogether. Looking at him, you decided, "That's a capital fellow, a merry fellow to be with; why, I should like to be a friend of his!"'

The Irish peasant then, and of subsequent black years, was to Sir George a figure of pathos hard to match in history. When in England, just after his work as Pro-Consul had closed, he drew that figure, and its seeming doom, in tender words. Nay, he was feeling for all men so placed that no ray of hope dawned upon them from the cradle to the grave.

The Irish peasant could not press his children to his breast, with the knowledge of being able to leave them the very humblest heritage won from his toil. Fathers and children, they could merely hope to obtain the temporary use of a spot of land on which to exercise their industry.

And what was the reward of all this labour? Hardly enough could be retained, from the proceeds, to procure the meanest food, the most ragged of clothes. Denied all power of legislation, and of considering and providing for his own necessities, as a citizen, the Irish peasant had lost the citizen's faculty, had become paralysed. He succumbed, almost without a struggle, to the fate brought him by famine, bred of evil days. He died on the mountain glens, along the sea coast, in the fields, in his cabin, after shutting the door. He died of starvation, though sometimes food was near, for he had even lost the hunger sense of the wild beast.

It was a keen project with Sir George, in his last years, to re-issue from London his proposals on the problem of Ireland. He had not lost belief in the pamphlet, as a channel for spreading ideas. He liked it, as he liked a well-thumbed book which, being opened at a page, so remained, instead of shutting with a snap. And of his venture, which never came off, he meditated, 'Might it not do good? They don't seem, even now, to understand all these matters—the real human nature of them. You hear talk of politics when it isn't politics at all, but men and women and

children. Proceed on that principle and difficulties
will quickly disappear.' He sought to brush aside
any veil of words, of terms, which might confuse and
darken problems.

His study-story of some Irish estate, granted by
Queen Elizabeth to an English nobleman, showed
how language might determine history. He noted
there, a force at work that tended to cloud the mind
and influence the imagination, in considering such
affairs. The estate was called 'a princely property,'
and the new holder was the 'aristocratic owner of the
soil.' He had 'extensive lands in England;' perhaps
he had 'the most beautiful demesne' and 'the finest
mansion' in that country. If the Elizabethan land-
lord, planted in Ireland, drove along the high road, he
was described as the 'noble occupant of the carriage.'
Did he spend, on the improvement of his property, a
little of the wealth won by the toil, privation, and
suffering of others, why, he was credited with 'un-
bounded liberality.'

So, down the centuries, the effect being that
sympathy was involuntarily drawn to all this rank,
wealth, and ease. Similarly, by an unconscious process of mind, there disappeared from the public eye the
gaunt faces, the bent bodies, of those who gave to rank
the means of wealth and ease. Contemplating the
plight, to which the people of Ireland had fallen in his
soldiering days, Sir George Grey exclaimed, 'What
intellect and power were lost to the nation! What
must have been the yearnings and agonies undergone

D 2

by many noble minds, feeling capable of great things, perhaps even of rescuing their country from the misery in which it was sunk ! '

Remove such people to a new atmosphere in the Colonies, where their natural attainments could have just scope, and behold a fairy change ! They would yield leaders of citizenship, men capable of shaping nations and legislatures, the laws of which the Old World would be glad to copy. Sir George could place the fruit of history, what had come about, in the remote basket of his hopes.

From it there dated a reminiscence of Sir Hussey Vivian, his Commander-in-Chief in Dublin. Sir Hussey, who, with his dragoons, covered Moore's retreat on Corunna, knew Sir George's father in the Spanish Peninsula. Viewing the troublous Irish times, he had ordered that military officers should wear their uniform, whether on duty or not. Handsome, genial, popular with everybody, a born soldier ; this was Sir George's appreciation of the man with whom he had the following adventure :

' Accompanied by a brother officer I was strolling along in Dublin, neither of us in uniform, notwithstanding Sir Hussey's order. We were walking arm in arm when, on turning a corner, we espied him and his staff. What was to be done ? We did not relish the notion of being caught in mufti, and looked round for a door of escape. There was none, except flight, and we took to our heels.

' The same night we each had a message from Sir

Hussey, begging us to call upon him at eleven o'clock next morning. We knew what that meant. Sir Hussey had been too quick for our flight. A trifle shamefaced, we duly presented ourselves at his quarters, and he talked to us for being abroad in plain clothes.

'Our aspect of penitence won upon Sir Hussey. "If you had not bolted," he added after the lecture, "I'm not sure that I should have felt it necessary to summon you before me. But, frankly, I could not stand the notion that any of my officers should run away from me." There the matter amiably closed, and it was not till afterwards that I had an idea, which might have appealed to Sir Hussey's gift of humour.

'I should have advanced to him the plea that, at least, we ran away alone, not in better company. A twinkle would have shone in his eyes, for he eloped with the young lady who became his wife. He got her out of her home at Bath, through a window, and they were happy ever after.'

To end a day happily was a maxim with Sir George, since it meant wisdom for the morrow.

V

SOUTHWARD HO!

Now, the morrow called Sir George Grey, as it calls most, whether they hear it or no.

In him, boyish meditation had ever been braided by melancholy, a legacy of the shock with which his father's death burst upon his mother. As he grew up, this became a deep-seated pity for the suffering, wide and bitter, among the common people. His mother's care, his step-father's converse, fostered that feeling, and the service in Ireland, with its lurid emphasis of the misery he had seen in England, determined him in quite a definite way. A valley of despair moaned in his ear.

'Can nothing,' he reflected with himself, 'be done for this canker, this wretchedness? Not much, from the inside, it may be, for the evil has too firm a grip. But down there, in the far south, is a new world! Surely it has the secret of sweeter, freer homes; surely in those new countries lie better possibilities? Yes, there the future has its supreme chance, there is the field for a happier state of existence! All can be given a chance, and in the spacious view, it will be planting posts of an Anglo-Saxon fence which shall prevent the development of the New World from being interfered with by the Old World.'

It was an abounding moment at which to be taken into partnership for the carrying forward of the universe. Half the globe, as we are intimate with it to-day, was then unknown, and North-West Australia was a no-man's land, saving to the Aborigines. It was believed by geographers that a big river, artery to an immense area of Australia, must here drain into the sea. A Government expedition, as head of which Sir George Grey was selected, should determine this, and familiarise the Aborigines with the British name and character.

'It's odd,' Sir George said, 'to reflect that in the latitudes, for which we were bound, human beings were everywhere eating one another. There was a patch of settled civilisation at the Cape, a lighthouse beaming into those seas, and that was about all. The full glow had to arrive from the north, seeing that south of a line, drawn from the Cape to Australia and New Zealand, there was only the Antarctic wilderness.

'You had ice in such parts as the savage could not inhabit; bleakness eternal, with no promise of help in raising him to a higher life. Mostly, in the history of mankind, civilisation has grown in upon a country from several quarters. The contrary should be noted in respect to the lands, which, as we left Plymouth, seemed to us so attractive, so full of promise for generations yet unborn. We were to test that promise, and Darwin's *Beagle*, having brought him home from a voyage, was to bear us on another.'

Sir George already knew Darwin enough to be a frequent caller on him in London. They discussed evolution, and a host of subjects in which Darwin manifested an interest. Sir George's vignette of him was that he was one of the most amiable men it were possible to conceive. He was closely occupied with his own work, but that did not prevent him from being an informed observer of other things.

'Of the advantages of association with master intellects,' Sir George would say, 'I sought to make the best use. The three men who exercised most influence on me were Archbishop Whately, Sir James Stephen, and Thomas Carlyle, names which I revere. They denote characters who adorned the nation, and as for Carlyle, I can only describe him as a profoundly great figure. When I think of him, I immediately fly to Babbage, the inventor of the famous calculating machine. And I'm afraid I smile.'

The link lay in certain experiences which befell Carlyle and Babbage in the streets of London. The coincidence was notable, and, farther, Sir George thought it strange that each great man should have made him confidant. But he had delighted in receiving the confidences, proofs of their friendship, and with a mixture of gravity and amusement he had consoled the martyrs.

CARLYLE'S ORDEAL

'Being,' he entered upon the tale, 'once introduced to Carlyle's company, I think by Sir Richard
Owen, it was my delight, during any spell in London,
to visit him at Chelsea. Perhaps, as the matter has
been long under review, I may remark that, to an out-
sider, no want of harmony was apparent, in the relations
between Carlyle and his wife. You were not conscious of any element of that description ; assuredly I
was not, and I prefer to cling to that impression.
Carlyle would sit at the right side of the fire, through
an evening, I on his left, and we would talk on all
manner of topics. I should most accurately describe
our talk by saying that we philosophised. Or, we
might read a little ; he was a loving reader.

'Carlyle believed, with truth, that I had been
influenced by his teachings, and if only for that reason
he may have been rather fond of me. We lift our
hats to ourselves, as reflected in somebody else. I had
a regard for him as a man, I gladly looked up to him,
though that did not block out differences of opinion ;
and altogether we got on admirably. During one of
those fireside talks, he detailed to me an incident, which
quite hurt his feelings.

'He had a horse then, and was in the habit of
riding out for exercise, almost every afternoon. He
was never very artistic in his manner of dressing, and
for horseback he had a long and singular fur coat,
which enfolded his legs. Between Chelsea and
Maida Vale, some boys were attracted by this quaint
figure astride a horse. Not knowing in the least, who

41

it was, they shouted at Carlyle ; he spoke something to them in reproof and passed on.

'But next day, at the same place, there were the boys again, and not content with mocking Carlyle, they threw pebbles at him. He did not sustain any injury, but he mentioned the matter to me with a sore heart, as indicative of the condition of the youth of the country, for want of the better educational opportunities, of which he was so earnest an advocate.

'As to Babbage, also a very gifted mind, he had Saturday evenings at home, and a person invited to one, was welcome ever after. His warfare against street musicians is history, and what I have to tell is one campaign of it. A German band was in the habit of annexing a position before his house, and treating him to its music. He might be deeply immersed in his work, when up would come this band, a trying disturbance to him. To be quit of the musicians he gave them money, with the inevitable thanks that they returned, seeking to be paid again, in order to depart once more.

'Babbage got tired of that sort of thing, refused to fee the Germans any longer, and ordered them to go and play somewhere else. They refused, and he, worn out by their music, left his study to seek a policeman and have them moved on. Like Carlyle, he dressed quaintly, and, moreover, at the moment, he was bareheaded. Not seeing a policeman, from his doorstep, he walked into the street to search for one.

'Babbage's dispute with the band soon collected a

small crowd, eager to witness the fun. It is
impossible for me, to say if those forming it, knew
the mathematician or not. That would depend on
the elements of the gathering, whether local or
casual, and who can determine the point in a
city like London ? A crowd gathers and disperses
here, as the wind plays with a volume of dust on a
March day. But, anyhow, the onlookers favoured the
band against Babbage, and they let their views be
understood, by pelting him with mud. Still, he held
to his purpose, routed out a policeman, and had the
band driven off. That time, at all events, he was able
to resume his calculations without molestation.'

It was a far cry, from these home-keeping transac-
tions, to that outermost fringe of British dominion for
which Sir George Grey found himself sailing :

> What time with hand and heart aglow
> The sower goeth forth to sow.

The cabin Darwin had occupied on the clumsy
Beagle, was his home from Plymouth to the Cape.
Instead of sleeping in a bunk he swung a hammock,
which he regarded as the better sea-going bed.
Though no yacht in heels, the *Beagle* had her own
qualities for rough weather, and she behaved loyally
towards her passengers. All the water supply had to
be carried in casks, with the effect, under a blazing
sun, that it soon grew bad. The ship called at South
America, where Sir George had his first revelation of
nature, as she blooms in the gorgeous tropics. The

colour, richness, luxuriance, dazzled him ; the more so that he had not read any description of the tropics, which adequately conveyed the sentiments they inspired.

He walked on shore of an evening, and the feelings engendered in him by the scene were wild, of a truth indescribable. He turned from the luxuriant foliage, to the stars aflame above, and he followed the fireflies as they danced. The woods were vocal with the hum of insect life, and balm loaded the breezes as they blew softly. These things at first oppressed his senses as so novel, so strange, that his mind almost hovered between the realms of fact and fancy.

'And you ask me of the sea,' he chatted ; 'to which I answer that it has always made an impression on me, best described as a mixture of awe and gladness. I was very conscious, during that long voyage by sail, of the presence and majesty of the Maker. I felt, standing on the deck of the *Beagle*, as if I were sur-rounded by some awful but beneficent power. The grandeur of the sea must make a reflective man religious, as its weirdness might breed superstition in the youthful, or the credulous.'

What wonder, he reasoned as he sailed, that a sailor should be superstitious ? He was separated in boyhood from his home, before he had forgotten the ghost stories of childhood. While the simple heart still loved to dwell upon the marvellous, he was placed amid all the marvels of the sea. In the dark, out of the howl of wind and din of waves, he would hear strange shrieks piercing the air. By him would float huge forms, dim and mysterious, from which fancy was prone to build strange phantoms. Ships might come and ships might go ; the sea must ever hold sway over the sailor man, a mistress to be loved and feared.

'Sailors,' he added, 'are not a religious class, so called, but I believe they are sincerely religious in their own manner. Poor Jack has faith that he is being guarded by some supreme power suited to the protection of the sailor. He does not seek to analyse that power ; he simply believes that it will attend him in the hour of peril. And that is how all nature's giant works affect you, when once you are clear of the help of man. You have a perfect reliance upon the unseen, and there follows a calm, sweet solace, which you cannot express. No doubts enter, when you are confronted with the great spirit, which seems to preside over virgin nature.

'But my emotions on the *Beagle* were as a flood. Here I was sailing to a quarter of the world which the Creator, in His goodness, had provided for the support and happiness of men. Yet they did not know actually what it was like ; the inheritance was still unexplored. And that land of North-West Australia was to be all my own, to designate as I wished. My feeling might be compared to that of a child waiting for a new toy. It gave rise to an ardent expectation.

'Behind was the despair of thousands, without the necessaries of life or the prospect of them ; a nightmare of darkness that haunted me. But in front, as I trusted, lay lands which should afford mankind another start. Why, the busy brains of England were already unconsciously preparing every device and implement, that could be useful to the rise of the New World. We make ready in the dark for the light.'

At Cape Town, the halfway house to Australia, Sir George chartered a schooner for detailed exploring work. In it, a trifle on the water, he completed a voyage which never lost its charm to him, notwithstanding the rude hardships. He wished to make all kind of inquiries into natural history, and when the weather fell calm he would go off in a boat and shoot sea-birds. Not the airy albatross, perhaps, for in it he realised the melody of motion, and it was not rare to naturalists. To shoot, from a boat, needed practice.

'You were,' he laid down the conditions, 'at issue with a heavy roll of the sea, even in glorious weather. Fortunately, I had always been an expert shot, and I quickly suited myself to the motion. You found your chances when the skiff sank into the trough of the waves, and a bird flew screaming over their tops ; or, again, when you rose on the surge and had a wider target.'

Thus at sea, and subsequently on land, he bagged many a fresh fact of natural history, and sent it home to enrich the British Museum. His word on that point was crisp. 'You had only to walk or row a little, and you secured a new living thing. The cry of the outlook was something discovered. The child waiting for the toy, of whom I spoke, was not half so happily situate as we. It was all surprises.'

His heart fell somewhat when he espied the land at Hanover Bay—the Promised Land, but naked and unkindly. What a contrast to the bouquet of Brazil ! Still, why should there not be acres rich and worthy, behind those dull grey rocks ? The idea of an incorrigible country was not to be entertained, for overcrowded England stood, with her hand for ear-trumpet, and the question on her tongue, 'What is the message ?' Adventure followed adventure in the effort to secure it.

'Somehow,' quoth Sir George, 'we didn't seem to mind the risks, and I imagine that is the experience of everybody who has encountered any. A man is zealous upon some task, it quite occupies him, and the dangers are just details. Afterwards, his friends make him out to be a bit of a hero, and he has leisure to fancy so himself, which is all entirely harmless. Now, I had to swim across an arm of the sea, where a violent tide ran, and where alligators and sharks had their haunts. The latter, I believed from observations made when we bathed off the schooner, could smell a human body in the water from a long distance. But the plain necessity was that, for the succour of certain members of the expedition, I must swim the lagoon.'

A nearer hazard furnished Sir George with a knowledge, which a call from his friend Sir Charles Lyell, the geologist, enabled him to use in fun.

Lyell walked in on him, in London, with a spearhead and the curiosity, 'How old do you judge that would be ?'

The weapon was of stone, uncouth, barbarous. 'A thousand years, eh ?' Lyell pursued.

Sir George let him go on for a while, then broke in, 'If that's a thousand years old, I likewise am a thousand years old, because one has been taken out of me.'

'What do you mean ?' was Lyell's ejaculation.

'Oh,' said Sir George, 'a head almost similar was on the spear which an Australian native drove into my thigh.'

Whereupon laughter, and tale of the fight.

VI

MAN AND NATURE ABORIGINAL

THERE never had been such a drama in that forest of
North-West Australia. The noise of the white man's
war fell upon the primeval silence, breaking it.

This battle dwelt acutely with Sir George Grey as
the single occasion, amid all his adventures, on which
he had been the instrument of taking human life.
He carried his own wounds to the grave, but only
sorrowed for the bullet he sped, though sheer necessity
drove it. The sacred light might burn in a savage,
ignorant of its nobler gleams, yet it was the gift of
the Creator. Moreover, Sir George's whole dealing,
towards native races, was guided by a pole-star
principle. The duty civilisation owed them, he
affirmed, was the larger in proportion to their state of
darkness. He held this to be the simple rule for the
Christian.

The natives of the Australian North-West were
a fine race physically, and, he judged, had an ingrain
of Malay blood. 'To see one for the first time,'
said Sir George, 'produced a great effect upon you.
These people were hardly known then.' They

coloured themselves in fearsome style, red being the favourite daub. No matter, the strangers from over sea would have greeted them gladly, being anxious to cultivate friendship. The wild men responded not; but hovered in the distance of the bush, or peered curiously from some covering of the rocks.

'I did everything I could,' Sir George remarked in that relation, 'to get acquainted with them, but at this period they would have nothing to do with me. Their fires might still be smoking, as we beat up a camping place, but they had left, suspicious of us. When travelling, I frequently had grave cause to be anxious lest we should be attacked, especially at night. Therefore, I made my men sleep a little apart from each other, in order that, if assailed, we might at least have some warning.'

It was full day when the assault did take place; otherwise Sir George would hardly have lived to describe it. He went back with spirit on the details, more armour of youth to be placed in the scabbard of age. One item held a small essay on the influences which determine human action in a crisis of life or death. He was speaking of the feeling that seized him when spear after spear cut into his flesh. Here was a struggle between mind and body, each determined to conquer—a study in the inner sanctuary; but how began the fight?

With two of his men, Sir George was on the march, notching trees by the way, so that the rest of the party could follow. At a turn they found themselves beset by a swarm of blacks, who had gathered in strength, determined to act against so small a force. Not many of the warriors could be seen at the outset, the rough ground sheltering them. But there they were, and in a most warlike humour.

A spear clove the air, singing their menace, as they yelled it in a hundred raucous voices. Scare shots, fired by Sir George, had no effect, not even when an incautious warrior was winged as an object-lesson. The Aborigines grew bolder, leaping hither and thither in the attack—evil spirits of the bush. The sight they made, all pigments, was expressed in the shout of one of Sir George's men, 'Good God, sir ! Look at them !'

The cry rose from behind a rock, where Sir George had ordered the man and his comrade to seek shelter. Fortunately, a series of rocks made a natural parapet to the right, and in a degree in front. Sir George, his gun empty at the moment, placed himself on the exposed left position. The spears rained round him, as if they were falling from the clouds. Things could not go on thus for long, and the natives planned to end them.

A superbly built fellow, lighter of skin than his companions, arrogant of air, showed to the front, evidently a general in command. He clambered, shouting the lust of battle, on to the summit of a rock, not more than thirty yards from the spot where Sir George lay. Then he swung a spear, with agile trick, and it grazed the hem of the white captain's coat. It would have done more had not Sir George by instinct, which is ever alert, jerked himself free of its path. Another spear, from the same supple hand, just missed his breast, striking the stock of his gun. This was too near for comfort and the future well-being of the expedition.

Sir George passed his empty gun to the English-man handiest, with the direction 'Please re-load it.' He had tried to do that himself, but his cramped position made it difficult to ram home the powder and ball. For his own gun, he snatched an unshot one which the man was struggling to release from its cover. In the hurry, piece and cover got entangled, but, with a wrench, Sir George tore the two apart. His plan of campaign was settled; he advanced to the rock where the light-coloured native had head-quarters. In bold initiative, there remained the only hope for Sir George and his following, against imminent massacre. Would it be a moral victory, won by a simple advance on the rock, or would it be necessary to strike? He had hesitated, as yet, to shoot straight; and he trusted still to avoid that extreme measure.

Three strides in the open, and three spears had him square and fair, a rent archery target. The first struck his watch, denting it, the second caught the fleshy part of his arm, the third tore into his thigh. The Aborigines were skilled spear-men, and proving it by Sir George's impalement, they shouted triumph. The shock of the weapons drove him to his knees, but what stung him was the crow of the blacks.

'That,' he said, 'produced in me a heated anger, and I was in the fight as I had not been till then. Stung by their mockery, I pulled myself together and was on my feet again in a trice. A spear was still sticking in my thigh, and blood flowed freely from the wound. I dragged out the spear, covered the wound with my haversack, so that neither enemy nor friend might be aware of it, and once more advanced.'

The chief grew alarmed at this steady investment of himself, and showed it by brandishing a club, as if to convey, 'Just you come nearer and this will drum on your head.'

Sir George's faculties were so keenly edged that he noted, in this bravado, a common link of mankind, high and low, civilised and barbarian. As long as the chieftain had been sure of his skin, he flung spears and sang valiantly; but when alarm entered him, those deadly measures were replaced by a mighty show. On the surface there was vast play of battle, but inwardly quaking. And Sir George marched forward, his right hand gripping the gun hard, his lip quivering, his eye burning.

The injured physical man was triumphant over the peace-loving soul, and anyhow there must now be a lesson. Of all those lines of thought Sir George was not, perhaps, conscious in his peril, yet, fetching back, he could trace them as they had worked. Seeking a solution by measures not violent, he had been given sore spears, whereon his finger tightened at the trigger, and he was a wound automaton; fixed, stern, a fate on feet, bearing down upon the chief in the shelter of the rock.

The brandished club was no stop; no more did the skirmishing support of the clan bring pause to the oncomer. The black general bobbed quite behind his rock, considering the necessity of absolute retreat. Next, he snapped off quickly, dodging here and there, as the aboriginal plan was, to avoid a cast of spears. It was not suited to avoid lead.

Everything had occurred within the space of a few minutes; for such crises do, otherwise the tension would kill. The chief ran; a tall dark body, with many other bodies watching it. Sir George raised his gun and pointed it at the warrior, struggling to a shelter from which the attack could be renewed. Snap went the trigger. With a bullet, the marksman could shoot a greater seabird, by the head, at a range of a hundred yards. This bullet caught the black between the shoulders, and he fell with a thud and a groan. In Sir George, the physical being surrendered itself again to the intellect. The situation was saved, his wounds stung him no more to vindication—he was sorrowful, a-weary.

There was no sound after the echoes of the shot had died away, a spluttering funeral knell. Other natives, laying their spears aside, sprang from behind trees and rocks to the help of their fallen chief. Nobody would harm them; the magic had ceased. They raised him with the greatest solicitude, and bore him off. His head hung on his breast; he could just stagger.

Faint from loss of blood, Sir George watched the serpent-like procession twine itself into the inner depths of the forest. Having conquered, he had to console himself on the victory and bind up his own hurts. These made him so weak that he must send to the camp for assistance, and he awaited its coming, a loaded gun on his knee. The blacks assailed no more; instead, the birds sang in the sun, and he asked himself, 'Is it all a dream?'

'Why,' declared one of his men, helping him towards the camp, 'should you worry yourself over having shot that black fellow? If you hadn't, where should we all have been? and anyhow there are plenty more like him in the country.'

This comforter was himself to need comfort, by and by, on a less sombre subject. He dashed in upon Sir George, crying, 'Sir, I have seen the Old Gentleman,' and with his frame shaking as if he had. It was the Australian bat on midnight circuit, a strange serenade to the European. Another of nature's creatures was to figure amid circumstances which did hold cause for terror.

'It's curious,' Sir George mused, 'how we remember trifles of the long ago with preciseness, when often bigger events are blurred. I recollect, very well, a slight incident of the scene on the island of Dorre, off the north-west coast of Australia, when a storm caught us. In turn, I caught an old cormorant by the neck, and the bird was all we had for breakfast next morning. A most sedate character he was, trying hard to maintain a dignified attitude in face of a very tempest of wind. He wished to fly, but could not, the violence of the gale pinning him to the ground. That was his death, which we all regretted ; and I'm sorry to add that we were grudging enough to call him tough in the eating.'

This gale was preface to the great adventure of the second stage of Sir George Grey's Australian explorations. He was to have plenty of opportunity for the study of the Australian Aborigine, who, by and by, received him in better wise than at the point of a spear. Somewhere, an old crone felt inspired to hug and kiss him, in the belief that he was her own dead son, spun white, and back on earth. Having recruited from his earlier sufferings, he had gone by Perth, up the coast to Shark's Bay in an American whaler. He arranged to make a depôt of Bernier Island, in the region of Shark's Bay, and there, on a lovely day, he landed his stores, burying them for safety in the soil. Up blew this storm, three nights later, when the explorers laid hands upon the solitary cormorant of Dorre. Had they been on Bernier, instead, the spoil might have been a kangaroo, for it owned a special breed of that family.

But to Bernier Island, the larder, Sir George returned, having completed a section of exploration. He had a dread lest the gale might have ravished his stores during his absence. Accordingly, he took only one or two of his people with him when he went, full of anxiety, to the spot where the provisions had been buried. He did not desire to alarm the others, should affairs turn out ill, as indeed they did.

'O God, we are all lost!' This was the wail for Sir George's ears, as the spade made it clear that the food-stuffs, with a trifling salvage, had been uprooted and scattered by the storm. It was almost the pronouncing of a sentence of death upon the party, having regard to the desert country which surrounded them, and their distance from civilisation.

'I hadn't an hour to lose,' Sir George realised, 'so back we hurried to the main camp and I delivered the news, counselling calmness and courage. I added my decision that we must endeavour to make Perth in the whale boats we had with us. It was a forlorn chance.'

The boats strained in a boisterous sea, and ultimately flung the voyagers ashore, three hundred miles, in a direct line, from Perth. Never were men given a harder tramp than across those miles, so parched and barren that they hardly echoed the *koo-ee* of a native. Yet there was no succour, no hostel, unless they could be covered.

For a little while fair progress was made, then strength declined through want of food and water. Sir George Grey sought courage and consolation in the dog-eared New Testament which he had in his knapsack. The hymns his mother had taught him came back into his head and heart, true comforters.

The land where she dwelt swam dim before his eyes, but his courage found strength anew. He pushed on, with a small company, in order to send back relief for those unequal to a sally. It was the perishing to the rescue.

A bird shot, was welcome as manna from heaven, and a muddy water-hole the sweetest of discoveries. The dew was eagerly licked from shrubs and reeds while the sun lingered a-bed. Lips grew black, tongues swollen, eyes wild, and the hopeless cry was: 'Water, or we die.'

The native guide schemed to lead Sir George from the others, begging, when discovered, 'Yes, we two may be saved if we go on; the others are so weak that they can't walk.' The master cocked his gun until the guide had carried him back to the party. They moved Perth-ward, a stricken line of famished men, wondering dumbly what was to happen. Did they really care?

If the leader had cheering and example, what were these set against this final ordeal: a blistering thirst of three days and two nights? Happily a water-hole, not bereft of all moisture, was found in the nick of time. A few birds flew about it in the evening, but Sir George Grey's hand shook so that he could take no aim. He headed a last desperate spurt for Perth; the reaching of succour, or the arrival of death. Which would it be?

How attractive to lie down and rest for ever on the parched grass, with some thin bush to keep off the sun. In the other extreme a shepherd of the hills, caught in a snowstorm, folds him in his plaid and goes to the sound sleep. Life in those wrestlers for it had sunk low; better die than hang on to a mere tether of living. Yet the better instinct asserted itself. And the second half of the expedition, far in the rear, cried for relief. On, on!

Sir George staggered across the miles until, in the goodness of fortune, he met natives who gave him food and water. He crawled into Perth, black with the sun, bones from want; he was not recognised by friends. A Malay, daft but harmless, led a vagrant life at Perth, getting bit and sup from the open tables of the colonists. The good wife of the outermost settlement, where Sir George Grey knocked, seeking refreshment, took him for 'Magic.'

'When I spoke to her in English,' he said, 'she looked so surprised that I feared she might run away, leaving me without the food and drink I needed. However, she merely exclaimed, "Well, if you're not 'Magic,' who are you?" Being told, and in time convinced, she brewed Sir George the most delicious cup of tea he ever drank. Soon, relief to the expedition was scurrying across the plains.

At the start of the journey Sir George had his sextant, but, having to walk hungry and thirsty, he needed to walk light. Therefore he hid the sextant in a tree, where, many a year later it was found, a rustic relic, by some settlers. Death raced him so hard that he eased the burden of keeping in front of it by tearing the boards from his New Testament. To the Word itself he clung impregnably.

The perils of Sir George Grey, as an Australian explorer, match some of those experienced by Captain Sturt. That brought up the name of the latter, and Sir George passed the eulogy : 'Australia owes to Sturt a greater debt, perhaps, than to any other of her explorers. His discoveries, apart from their own stir and colour, were of the first importance in the successful settlement of the country. I knew him well ; a man who would do anything for anybody, and never think of his own interests.'

Admiring Sturt so heartily, Sir George, with others, had urged that the honour of a title should be conferred upon him. He died in England before actually receiving it, 'Whereupon,' said Sir George, ' I next suggested that his widow should have the rank which otherwise would have been hers, and from that, I judge, sprang the very proper rule now obtaining in such a case.'

VII

PLANTING THE BRITON

'I ALWAYS got what I wanted in life,' Sir George Grey made arch comment on himself, 'and many things, also, that I did not want.'

His appointment as Governor of South Australia, with the steps leading up to it, he could group under the first head. His explorations had shown that no great river, no second Murray, drained the North-West area of Australia. This was information for geographers, and he had more, since, to quote his own words, 'We learned as much about the region, in a general way, as was necessary.' Next, he acted for a while as Government Resident at King George's Sound, and he investigated the country thereabout.

'The settlement of King George's Sound,' he said, 'was quite small, and I discharged all the duties of the State. I don't remember that I fined anybody; just decreeing: "Oh, you must make up your disputes yourselves." Perth, now so grown, was at that date a mere townlet. It had few people, ships called rarely, and practically it was shut off from the world.'

This was the brand-new Australia. Beside it, there is a glimpse of olden England, in the manner Sir George Grey was bid to be Pro-Consul. A special messenger pelted down to Bodiam, where, after his return to England, he had been staying for a month, the hero of his relatives. The messenger brought the other London news that the guns of the Tower had been firing, to announce the birth of the Queen's first child, the Princess Royal. Therefore his arrival caused a double commotion in the family circle, two notes of joy and gratulation. Sir George posted express to London, changing horses at short stages in order to make the better speed.

It was his supreme wish to serve the Colonies, and he had a glimmering notion that the chance would come. Still, he was at one of the crossings in a young man's life, when it is hard to know what the road is to be. He had always his commission in the army, but was that his definite signpost ? He sighed for a wider door of usefulness, and behold it opened ! That it should be open so soon, was, perhaps, remarkable, only the word was to be his constant accomplice.

'I had never met Lord John Russell, who made me the offer,' Sir George explained. 'He was going upon what little I had done, in regard to Australian affairs, especially a kind of despatch by me on native administration. After adequate thought, and acting upon good advice, I confirmed my first resolve to accept the Governorship of South Australia. It was, apparently, to be an onerous post.'

To Adelaide went this Queen's Governor, not yet thirty, his mission the undoing of a tangle ; for South Australia was on the verge of bankruptcy, almost before it had entered into business. Hardly an acre of land was in cultivation, and most of the people were in Adelaide with nothing to do, clamouring for food. Sir George perceived at once that they must be got on to the land. To have the settlers securely there, from the first, meant that they were to grow into a nation, not to amass temporary riches, and then return to an already overcrowded world.

Again, in South Australia, as elsewhere, he endeavoured to carry out what he regarded as a cardinal principle in the making of a new country. This was to draw capital direct from the soil, not by the raising of too heavy loans. How to rear a nation ? Keep its conditions of life natural, even simple ; make it self-creative and self-reliant, train it as if it were an individual. Let it build its national homestead, as a man might lay out his own little stance of ground. Then, the community would have the parents' love and pride towards all that had been created. Sir George put his shoulder to the wheel of the settlers' cart in South Australia, and shoved until the harvest drove home.

'I ascertained,' he spoke of those efforts, 'that the soil was very suitable for wheat, and we sowed widely. The crop, vital to the Colony, depended upon the weather. Would there be enough rain ? I often crawled out of bed in the morning, while it was half-dawn, to ascertain if there was any promise of rain for that day. The wheat was at the critical stage, and if I had made the weather, it could not have proved more suited in its conditions.

'It was the first extensive wheat crop of South Australia; the first harvest-home of the bunch of people, who had there been shaken on to the sea beach. When the wheat had ripened, everybody—including, I am glad to say, the Governor—turned to the harvesting of it. Riots had threatened earlier, the result of the state of affairs in the Colony, and the measures which I deemed it necessary to introduce. As a precaution, I had some soldiers, about a hundred and fifty I think, sent to me from New South Wales. That was a step on which I was entitled to congratulate myself. At the pruning hook, in getting in that harvest, they were of vast assistance, and not often have soldiers been more nobly occupied.'

Yet the pruning hook, which Sir George associated with the historic harvest, and with Ridley, an early Australian colonist, was hardly of the Scriptural pattern. It was a subtle machine, invented for a harvest where the wheat-ears were needed, not the straw. The former were chopped off, collected in a sort of trough, and the straw was burned for manure. Here was waste, only there was no avoiding it, and, moreover, the meaning of 'waste' is defined by circumstances. The South Australian soil was so fruitful that it only needed to be thrown seed. Sir George satisfied

himself that it contained gypsum, such as belongs to
the fertile parts of Egypt.

Thus gypsum reared wheat, under the footprint
of the black man, who shod his spear in obsidian.
Things that began before history, were meeting from
very different sides. Nature extended one hand to
the inflow of civilisation, another to the rude holding
of it back. There was a point of contact in the
adventure of a settler, Turner by name, whom Sir
George Grey met near the Murray River. It fell
out comedy, but might have been tragedy; and how
often those two flirt with each other round a corner!

The fact, upon which the affair hinged, was that
Turner wore a wig, no doubt for sufficient reason.
He was making a journey across country, and with
him were a few natives, guides and packmen. Perhaps his head grew hot; anyhow, at some stage he
took a penknife from his pocket, and ran the blade
under the edge of the wig. The native nearest to
him, suspicious of witchcraft, stared at this act, terror
written on every feature.

With a deft lift of the knife, Turner had the wig
clear of his head. The native stayed no longer to
consider 'Is this a sorcerer?' He whipped off, to
what he considered a safe distance. The innocent
Turner followed his retreat with laughing eye, amused
at the effect produced. For acknowledgment, a spear
cracked through the satchel on his back, and wounded
him slightly. His load had saved his life, and he
warily resumed the wig.

The quality of the early settlers in South Australia, gave Sir George Grey great trust in the new Anglo-Saxondom to be built up in the south. Many of them were Nonconformists, which suggested to him the Puritan founding of New England. As a body they had a worth, a sincerity, a true ring which could not fail of fine records. That knowledge helped him, in the difficult task of setting South Australia on its feet. His policy of severe economy made shoes pinch, but he held on, ever ready with the courteous word for those who most assailed him.

He could contrast Adelaide, when town sites went at auction for about five pounds an acre, with the Adelaide of our day. 'If you had yourself,' somebody put it to him, 'invested in a few of those sites, you would be rich instead of poor?' The remark bore partly upon the enormously enhanced value of city lands all over Australia, partly upon Sir George's simple unconcern for wealth, his disregard of mere money. He was almost inclined to pity millionaires, as being among the afflicted. The tinkle of gold was never in his golden dreams.

'Yes,' he answered, 'the land which sold for five pounds in Adelaide, might, at the present moment, be worth nearer five thousand. Throughout my career, I followed a very strict rule in those matters. I never had any dealings in land, or other property, except as Governor, charged with the interests of the whole community. My despatches were my sole title-deeds.'

'There is no virtue,' he laid down, 'in honest duty, such as we claim from every public servant. Our lofty ideal in that regard, is true British wisdom. Moreover, need a man, estimating wealth on its merits, care to be rich ? What private means I inherited, I have spent largely on public ends. I mean, in particular, those libraries at Cape Town and Auckland, which I was enabled to help. Why, the bargain is all mine ; I am the debtor for the opportunity.'

To Sir George Grey, Oceana had seemed a fertile land, crying across the depths, 'Come unto me, all ye that labour and are heavy laden, and I will give you rest.' His mission was to pass that invitation freely to the shores of the Old World, and to be vigilant on the spot, keeping a clear ring. He did not want folks to come, only to find a path strewn with the obstacles and ills they thought to have left behind. His purpose was to make life as generous, as unfettered as possible. Keep the Old World out of the New ! It became a passion with him ; and he counted on making the New World an influence towards regenerating the Old. The line, in respect of both aims, was to retain the control of the New World for the Anglo-Saxon. That meant freedom, because the non-intrusion of arrayed nations, which would hinder it.

When Greece needed a king, Sir George Grey was mentioned as one with likely parts for the post. 'I should think,' wrote Freeman the historian, 'he would be just the man to deal with any unruly

clements in the country.' The absolute offer of the
crown of Greece, would not have tempted Sir George
for an hour.

As he said seriously, while joking on the point,
'In the far south there was literally nobody to lead,
whereas Greece had men sufficient to mould her
destinies. Anyhow, one given the administration
of Greece, would not have had a work more honourable than the development of Australasia, a larger
business altogether. Here was a region where several
kingdoms were in the raising, where the pattern could
take something from yourself. What drew me to
the far south, as a fairy-tale might, was that charm,
"Yes, it's all new. Hardly anything has yet been
done. It's mine to do with as I will."'

There was the white man's history to fashion, and
the black man's history to discover. Sir George did
not neglect the second inquiry, because the other was
the more important. His explorations had given him
the idea that Australia was of a volcanic origin.
He judged it to have been, at some period, a series
of islands, each with its own volcano. These islands
had risen from the sea, been licked into shape
probably by earthquakes, and coming gradually together, had formed a continent. During his Governorship of South Australia, Sir George fell upon
a piece of evidence which materially supported this
belief. The skeleton of a whale, as Sir Richard Owen
certified the specimen, was discovered quite inland,
beyond the first mountain range. If Sir George

had arrived at some view, after long deliberation, he liked it to be accepted, as we all do. Therefore he welcomed the discovery of that whale.

'I was laughed at,' he commented, 'when I insisted that the natives of Australia must have come from a race more civilised than themselves. A variety of reasons supported my estimate of their origin ; as that, all over native Australia, there appeared to prevail a rigorous law governing marriage.

'It demonstrated that the natives understood the effect which blood kinship would exercise upon the stamina of a race. There was no single great tribe in Australia, but a series of tribes ; yet this law was general among them. No conqueror could have imposed it ; instead, it must have sprung from a family coming in, and bringing it with them. Where did that family come from ? I cannot tell. But we see, among the Aborigines of Australia, customs resembling those of the African continent.'

Studying those customs, Sir George had been witness of the ancient rite of circumcision, which also argued a higher civilisation. The blacks built themselves, layer upon layer into a human altar, and on it the sacrifice was performed. Meanwhile a grunting noise, 'Ha-ha-ha,' sonorous, even solemn, a savage mass, arose from the heap. Sir George imagined that he was almost the first Englishman to behold this ceremony, on the part of the Aborigines of Australia. To them it was religion ; whence did they get it ?

Their common rule Sir George found expressed as

an eye for an eye, a tooth for a tooth, but they had their lighter moments. He discovered, in a lady savage, a humorous link between the vanity of all womankind. There had been a native dance, and he was leaving, when the chieftainess approached him with the request, 'Oh don't go away until you have seen my son dance; he will be beautiful!'

'I waited, of course,' Sir George consented, ever gallant, 'and the son presented himself, daubed over with dirt of divers colours, and began to hop about. He was well built, he danced cleverly, he cackled in his finery, and his mother was hugely proud of him. She might have been an English duchess, introducing a pretty daughter to a first ball. It was seeing the parent in the child, the most marked form of self-flattery. Actually, tears of joy ran down those black, wizened cheeks. I wouldn't have had it otherwise, and I was glad I stayed for the young buck.'

Wherever Sir George Grey went in Australia, he found the natives living from hand to mouth, on roots and the rewards of the chase. They were equally primitive, in a system of punishment, which stood an offender up as a mark for spears. But they were sportsmen, for it was prescribed that the quarry must only be chastened in the legs. The tribes also reached out to civilisation, in that each had its ground marked off, with the accuracy of a European estate.

'I believe'—Sir George carried this subject wider —'that the cardinal trouble in the settlement of new countries, has lain in the desire of the white man to possess the lands of the black man. Perhaps it has been inevitable, but the thing should be done on a proper method, and that has not always obtained.'

Sir John Franklin, at Van Diemen's Land, was a brother Australian Governor to Sir George Grey, but they never met. 'I had correspondence with him,' Sir George observed, 'and from all I heard he was a most interesting personality. Subsequently, I did meet Lady Franklin, who had much character, allied to womanly gentleness. Everybody admired her loving persistence to unravel the fate which had overtaken her husband in the Arctic regions.'

It was almost a discovery to Sir George, with his wide knowledge of Australasia, that he had never set foot in Tasmania. He passed it variously, on board ship, yet had not been ashore. How was that?

'Maybe,' he replied, 'because all my life I made it a rule, not to let anything turn me aside from what I had immediately in hand. If you set out for a place, with some definite object in view, your road should be the most direct one. Don't branch off, because there is something elsewhere which might gratify your curiosity.'

Sir George disciplined the hours, holding himself accountable for them to his fellow-men and to the Great Accountant.

VIII

PICTURES IN BLACK AND WHITE

THERE had been a reception in London, by Gladstone,
following the usual dinners which ministers of the
Queen give in honour of her birthday.

To Sir George Grey, who was in the splendid
crowd, came the wife of an eminent member of the
Government, carrying to an old friend a woman's
eager news of her own dinner.

'Oh,' she whispered in that still small voice
which rises a clarion note above a general buzz, 'oh,
everything went off admirably, and Bob's delighted.
But the soup was just a little cold.'

The soup often got cold at the Governor's board
in Adelaide, the while he was laying the foundations
of the Colony. This implied study of the problem,
'How are we to utilise the natives for the civilisation
which has begun to invade them in Australia, New
Zealand, and South Africa ?'

Already, in Western Australia, Sir George had
devoted earnest study to the subject, and method
ripened with him. He felt, perhaps, that he had been
given a unique work, in the sense of moulding raw

human materials to higher ends. He was a master craftsman, and as he contrived, so there might be issues near and remote. The future dwelt with Sir George when to others, lacking the seer's eye, it was still below the farthest horizon. Call it the second-sight of statesmanship—something which is born with a person rather than acquired. He had simple words for the ideas that underlay his life's labour, in bringing barbarous races under the harrow of cultivation.

'It is quite evident that man's great line of exertion, is towards getting more food for himself and his family. This truth applies to him in all his states; only the more he advances in material welfare, the more he needs to satisfy him. With a savage, mere food is enough, but in the centres of civilisation beautiful clothes, fine horses and carriages, marble palaces, all form the prize. Ever, it is the same impelling desire.

'Well, the way to adopt with natives, was to show them how to obtain more food. Benefit them in that manner, and they would regard you as their friend, and you would have influence over them. I always paid a native, doing unskilled work, the wage a white would have received for the same effort. It was mere justice. Yet, so small a thing had immense results, for manhood was cultivated in the black. Self-respect infected him. He discovered himself, with proud surprise, to be a man instead of a chattel.

'The mystery of managing native races, resolves itself into a few natural laws. My hardest trouble was the witchcraft, which held in bonds, the savage peoples whom I had to govern. It might differ, here or there, in its characteristics; the evil was there all the same. Not merely did the natives believe in witchcraft, having been swathed in it for ages, but their chiefs made a profit therefrom, and were staunch for its maintenance. My antidote was the introduction of medical aid, so that in the cures wrought, those children of the dark, might see what surpassed their own magic. They were discomfited, as it were, on their own ground.

'Superstition, which I distinguish from witchcraft, though the greater evil flourished on the less, had its best treatment in the spread of the Christian religion. Surely, a wonderful witness of its divine origin, lies in the fact that it applies to the elevation and happiness of all the world's races, is understandable to all. Farther, native schools made advances upon sheer ignorance, as hospitals did in respect to witchcraft; and it was possible, in some measure, to eradicate native indolence by affording youths a training in a trade, or grown men work on public improvements. Here we return to where we began—food as the primitive impulse driving mankind.'

No trait of human nature was neglected by Sir George Grey, in his exertions to plant the better ideas of living. He detected that the Kaffirs of South Africa were sharp to humour, owners of a lively sense of the ridiculous. On that hung an incident, which brought out the value of the personal equation in dealing with natives, whether in South Australia, New Zealand, or South Africa. It was an item of Sir George Grey's whole native policy. An old witch doctor, he mentioned, had been inciting unrest among the dark masses of Kaffraria. Sir George had him put comfortably in prison, where he could be certain of medical attendance and rest. That was the least office, demanded towards a human being evidently in a disturbed state of health.

It confounded the witch doctor. Never was there such a father to his people as Sir George Grey, and the tribes of a hemisphere acclaimed it. The witch doctor had his doubts, took his physic wryly, and begged piteously to be set free. He was released, on the strict promise that he would cease being a firebrand. Not that alone, for he publicly recanted among the Kaffirs, gathered on a market morning, to their huge amusement and derision. He made no more trouble, and could not, had he tried, his fame being ruined.

'A joust of fun like that,' was Sir George Grey's moral from the incident, 'had a wonderful effect upon natives. It was much better than shooting the witch doctor, and quite as effective. Even among whites, ridicule may be a very serious punishment.'

But the Pro-Consul was not always warranted to win, in his encounters of wit and wisdom. He put to the debit account, a dialogue he had with a batch of Kaffir chiefs, on the proper employment of their moneys. He wondered if the wages, earned from native work on the roads, and in cultivating the lands, were always wisely spent. The broad inquiry was well enough, as the chiefs took it, but unfortunately Sir George went on to state a case in proof.

'For instance,' he innocently pleaded, 'is it necessary that so much should be expended on the jewellery and ornaments of the women ? Would they not really look more handsome, without all those gew-gaws of brass and metal, which they wear round their arms and ankles ?'

An aged chief rose and gravely replied, ' You are a great chief, Governor, and you have done marvellous things. You have persuaded us to labour, yea, to make roads which we knew would lead to the conquest of our country. But you had better rest and be content, not allowing success in other things to in-duce you to enter upon what no man can accomplish. If you attempt, O Governor, to wage war with woman and her love of ornament, you will assuredly fail.'

' The assembled chiefs,' Sir George wound up the tale, ' roared with delight at this answer, which really left me without a word to say.'

In South Australia he established one of his first schools, and the lessons obtained from it were widely useful. They suggested the difficulties that had to be overcome, wherever the alphabet was spread before the Aborigine. Children made bright pupils, but, as they grew up, were apt to go back on what they had learned. The reason was not far to seek. An educated native found himself out of touch with his uneducated fellows ; education made a barrier. He was not the equal of the Europeans, and could form no friendships with them. Neither was he happy with his own people, whom he had passed in civilisation. He swung between two poles, and very frequently was dragged back into the volume of native life.

'You see the difficulty,' Sir George pointed out, 'as one that is necessarily present with regard to all savage races. But it has its cure, which I put into practice, namely, to provide males and females with an equally good education. Especially, I mean a technical education, the learning of some trade or art, for that was all important. Natives, on leaving school, could then make a living by plying among the Europeans the industry they had learned. Should a native learn shoemaking, he could find a wife in a girl trained to domestic service. Such a couple were not compelled to return to their own people, and they were independent of the Europeans. It was lifting a race by its two halves, these being essential to each other, not leaving one of them behind.'

Next, a picture in black and white. It wandered into the gallery of Sir George's Pro-Consulship in South Australia. At the entrance to Spencer's Gulf lies an island, on which a fortuitous little colony had established itself. The colonists were mostly escaped convicts, from the penal settlements of Australia and Van Diemen's Land, or sailors who had deserted their ships. The men killed the seals which frequented the island, trading in their skins with vessels that now and then called for the purpose.

'I had never judged it my business,' Sir George spoke of this matter, ' to interfere with those sealers. They kept the peace among themselves, and did not come into contact with the settlement at Adelaide. Indeed, they had some form of justice, under which a member who did anything wrong, was transported for a time to a smaller neighbouring island. There he could live on oysters of a sort, and on fish caught with lines supplied to him. It was being sent to Coventry, new style, including oysters, which, like all delicacies, will, I suppose, cause surfeit.

' The chief of this settlement, as he might be termed, had brought a native woman with him from Van Diemen's Land. He was fairly educated, not without considerable power of reasoning, and I had repeated talks with him. Most of his companions had Australian black women living with them, and there was a story that these had been taken by force from the mainland. The natives of Van Diemen's Land were entirely distinct from the natives of Australia, and the differences have been much debated. The hair of a Van Diemen's Land woman was curly and woolly, Kaffir like ; that of the Australian woman long and straight.

' Very well, I was anxious to obtain a genuine specimen of the Tasmanian female's hair. It would, I believed, be valuable to posterity, as bearing upon the divergences of two neighbouring races. Of course, the Tasmanians have now been extinct for years, and their disappearance was then rapidly approaching. It was best, to prevent any doubt, that I should myself cut the tress of hair from the woman's head. The chief of the colony, in response to my request, said he was quite willing that she should visit Adelaide for this purpose. She was agreeable herself; curious as to the scenes, strange to her, which she might witness in Adelaide. As we are all born hungry, so we are all born curious; merely we differ in degree. In due time she arrived, and I secured the necessary sample of her hair, which remains, probably, in the Auckland Museum.

'Delighted with a new stock of clothes, the woman left Adelaide on her return to the island, this also having been arranged. She was to light a fire on a crag of the mainland, at which signal her lord and master would put over with his boat to fetch her. Now recur my conversations with him, which included the question, " Is it not rather bad that you should all be living here with these native women ? "

'His answer, coming from such a quarter, surprised me, and proved him a regular controversialist. " It does nobody harm," he argued, " and we are much more comfortable than we should otherwise be. There was nothing hasty in what we did ; every step was taken deliberately. Knowing we could not re-enter the world, and there being no settlers, then, in these parts, we considered : Could we not found a small nation ourselves ? The greatest nation of ancient times, cast in very similar circumstances, did not feel it wrong to carry off, by force, the females of another people. Thus, they acquired women to look after their homes, while otherwise they would have been living in a pitiable state, with no ties. What that nation did, we have done." Such was the word of the island chief, and no appeal, in justification, to history, could ever have been made in stranger circumstances.

'Was it not,' Sir George felt, 'extraordinary to hear the case of the Romans and the Sabine women, pleaded in defence of a tiny outlawed community, situate on the wild Australian coast, where another empire, more magnificent even than that of Rome, was just planting itself? The thing almost swept one's mind from the question itself—a difficult one to answer as submitted.'

Then, in this odd affair, the untutored far south was springing to the support of Sir George's views as to cause and effect. Imitators of ancient Rome, on an island of Spencer's Gulf, Australia, many centuries later! The theory of the universe, expressed as 'cause and effect,' had been borne in upon Sir George from the moment he turned thinker. It was a favourite text between him and Babbage, into whose ear he poured his reasonings.

'Subjects occurred to me,' he said, 'which I believed had not been given sufficient prominence, and this was one of them. I fancy Babbage wrote about it.'

Every motion, every word spoken, they agreed,

abode an eternal influence in the world. Nothing, either in action or in reasoning, was lost; the unborn ages made response. If we could go back far enough we should be able to trace, by the influence it had wrought, that red streak, the murder of Abel. Had we a divine intellect, we could see the whole universe, a complete machine, at work. Sir George would marvel at the splendour of that creation, asking himself, 'Might it, if fully revealed, not be all too dazzling for human eyes ?'

The Aborigine—Australian, Maori, and Kaffir—was to him a guarantee, by physical evidence, of the same law of the universe. They three had passed intimately before him, and he had mapped the intertwine of their paths. These were noteworthy, being a fruit of Sir George's observation on the human race in primitive lands. First, consider the women, who, among barbarians, not having animals of burden, had always been pack horses.

'In New Zealand,' he said, 'with its forests, the females had to carry their loads along narrow paths. The proper way to carry a pack is on the head, but the trees made that impossible. Hills, too, had often to be climbed, and to ease the ascent a bending posture must be taken. Add that fact to the load on the back, and it was a consequence that Maori women should evolve clumsy figures.

'In Australia there was more open ground, and in many parts the method was to carry a load on the head. Thus, the native women were better of figure, though quite unequal to their lithe, graceful Kaffir sisters of South Africa. Here the country was free and open, and the carrying of a weight on the head naturally followed.'

Second, the men of those races.

'The Australians,' Sir George went on, 'were hunters, and had to climb trees in search of opossums. They drove holes into the trunks with their stone axes, dug in their big toes, and ascended. Such efforts provided them with long legs, while, again, they walked with turned-in toes. Why? Having scrub to penetrate, they must cut roads through it—a tiresome labour, not pursued more than was necessary. If they turned in their toes, they could sidle along a mere bee-line of clearing.

'The Maoris were very short in the limbs, this arising from the amount of time they spent in their canoes. Peculiarities of environment equally distinguish the Kaffirs, who were the most agile of the three races. Set against any of the others, all in the primitive state, the Kaffirs might have prevailed, though who could say? Neither the Maoris, nor the Australians, worked in iron weapons, while the Kaffirs did, and that circumstance would have told, in the clash of prevailing or going down.'

Contrasts were sharp in Oceana when she was young, which entitles you to pass quickly from Sir George Grey's careful estimate of the native races he ruled, to a little romance of South Australia. A Highland settler, with the Highland name McFarland,

lived in a cottage some twenty miles from Adelaide.
He was an informed and interesting Scot, and when
the Governor was tired, he would ride over to his
shieling and stay a day or two.

'A number of German colonists,' Sir George's
narrative on this proceeded, 'had come to South
Australia, seeking to improve their condition. Labour
being scarce and highly paid, the German girls went
out and did shearing. They moved from farm to farm,
accompanied by some of the older women, and at
night they would be housed by the settler who
happened to be employing them.

'Among the shearers was a girl who had a
great reputation for beauty. She was quite a belle,
and so winning that everybody liked her. One
morning old McFarland rushed in upon me at
Adelaide, in a state of high excitement. His nephew,
a genuine McFarland also, had, the previous night,
eloped with the German beauty. The uncle was
indignant that the nephew should run away with a
foreigner—yes, a foreigner ! He implored me to send
the police to search for them, but I replied that I
could do nothing. He must go to the Justices of the
Peace and petition, if he wished to take action, on
which point I offered no advice.

'Scarcely had he left, when the relatives of the girl,
escorted by the German pastor, invaded me, full of an
equal indignation and also demanding the police. I
could only repeat the answer I had given to McFarland,
even when it was pleaded that the girl, like other

G 2

members of the German community, had pledged herself not to marry outside it. It was urged that anything she might do to the contrary would not count, but that argument would not hold. We heard, by the evening, of the marriage of the runaways.

'They had been united by some Justice of the Peace, a frequent occurrence then, there being few ministers, and the match proved a happy one in every respect. How the bold young McFarland managed to carry off his bride from her custodians I never learned, and I suppose I did not inquire.'

Only in a South Australia, rescued from the chasms, grown stalwart under the hand of Sir George Grey, could there have been such a romance. It needed a stout heart and a trustful, loving one, and these are the characteristics of a healthy community.

IX

OVER-LORD OF OVER-SEAS

THE war song of Lamech, father of Tubal Cain, called Sir George Grey hurriedly to New Zealand. The Maoris were exploiting the legacy of the first artificer in brass and iron.

> Adah and Zillah, hear my voice ;
> Ye wives of Lamech, hearken unto my speech :
> For I have slain a man to my wounding,
> And a young man to my hurt.
> If Cain shall be avenged sevenfold,
> Truly Lamech seventy and sevenfold.

In this genesis of verse, Sir George also found the noise of all combat with skilled weapons. A cry of sorrow and repentance by Lamech, at some ill-starred act, which filled him with remorse ? Surely, rather the exultant note of a rude spirit, handling mastery anew in the ingenuity of his son.

There stood Lamech, on the edge of creation, crowing over the cunning forces Tubal Cain had discovered. 'I have slain a man to my wounding, and a young man to my hurt !' It was to be a long roll. Sir George would recite the lines once, twice, yet again, and the thunder tramp of a Maori impi sang in his ears.

'The story of my going to New Zealand,' he thought, 'may appear quaint in these days, when the cable anticipates all pleasant surprises. We had heard at Adelaide, through a coaster arriving from Sydney and Van Diemen's Land, also from a British man-of-war on the Australian station, of serious fighting in New Zealand. A friend of my own was in command of the warship in question, which had put into Adelaide for supplies. I spoke to him of events in New Zealand, the heavy slaughter of British soldiers, and the evident critical situation. I had no distinct authority to order his vessel to New Zealand, but I felt it to be a wise step. Accordingly, I wrote him a letter saying he ought to proceed to the scene of trouble, and that I was prepared to assume the responsibility. We got together what materials of war were available in South Australia, and what money we could spare from the Treasury of the Colony. So furnished, he sailed for New Zealand.

'A few days later, I was out riding with my step-brother from England, who was on a visit to me at Adelaide. We were cantering along a road near the coast, when a man with a light cart stopped us. An unknown ship had been sighted before we left Adelaide, and this man came from the quarter where she had taken up anchor. He stated that it was the *Elphin-stone*, belonging to the East India Company, that despatches had been brought for me, and that he had them in his cart. He added that the *Elphinstone* had come to take me away, and that some of the officers would very likely be landed by the time I got to the place of anchorage. This was all very puzzling. I jumped off my horse, sat down beside some trees, opened the despatch bag, and devoured its contents.'

It had been carried express from London, first overland to Suez where the *Elphinstone* awaited, and then by sea to Adelaide. The British Government, much alarmed as to affairs in New Zealand, borrowed the *Elphinstone* from the East India Company. In effect, it was adopting the Suez Canal route, long before the Suez Canal existed. Not often, perhaps, did the Colonial Office, of the young Oceana period, have such a healthy attack of nerves. Also, it spoke of Sir George Grey handsomely in these despatches ; which was encouraging.

Noting his career as a whole, you seem to perceive the scales of official praise and disgrace rising and falling, like a see-saw. Now, he was being set to the straightening-out of some twist in Oceana, to the healing of a sore which threatened one of her limbs. Then, when Oceana, in that quarter, was waxing strong on his regimen, Downing Street, not having prescribed it all, would trounce him. The calls to South Australia, New Zealand, and South Africa were in the agreeable key. The other note piped in the good-byes to South Africa and New Zealand, and in the registered blue-book phrase 'a dangerous man.' It was the ancient, merry way of regarding the Colonies ; with, in conflict, a masterful Pro-Consul who, being on the spot, would there administer. Whether the see-saw had him up, or dropped him down, Sir George kept the good heart, as school-children do.

The tribute of Lord John Russell was that, in South Australia, he had given a young Governor as difficult a problem in administration as could arise. He pronounced the problem to have been solved with a degree of energy and success, hardly to be expected from any man. In New Zealand, Lord Stanley gave Sir George difficulties more arduous, duties even more responsible. The ability they demanded, the sacrifices they involved, were their best recommendation to one of Sir George's character. ' Before I mounted my horse again, after reading the despatches,' he recalled his decision, ' I made up my mind to go to New Zealand. Indeed, I had not two opinions on the matter from the moment I became acquainted with the wish of the Colonial Secretary. It was a clear duty lying before me, and that is ever the light to steer by.'

He sailed for New Zealand in the *Elphinstone*, and retained her on war service there, another of his new departures. ' As far as I know,' he said, ' no East India Company's ship had previously been the consort, in active operations, of men-of-war of the Royal Navy. There was a row afterwards, as to paying for the *Elphinstone*, and I suppose I had no right to keep her. However, I realised that everything hung on how effective a blow I could at once strike in New Zealand.' Several men-of-war were at his orders, and later they were strengthened by the first steamer ever seen in these parts. It had come to New Zealand from the China station, and was a show alike to colonists and to Maoris.

A trifling incident of the naval activity, during the Maori wars, dwelt in Sir George's memory by reason of its droll comedy. An officer, thoroughly tired out, went to his bunk, leaving directions that he should be called at a particular hour. It happened that the awakening of him, fell to a blithesome midshipman having the sombre surname D'Eth. The sleeper turned himself lazily, half asleep, wishful only to be left to sleep on, and asked ' Who's there ? '

The midshipman held up the blinking, old-fashioned lantern which was in his hand, and answered ' D'Eth.' The weirdly lit cabin solemnly echoed the word, making its sound uncanny—' D'Eth ! '

' Good God,' the officer in the bunk exclaimed, sitting up with a jerk, as if the last trumpet had sounded : ' D'Eth, where ? '

Then he saw ' D'Eth ' grinning, realised that there was still time for repentance, and bundled forth to the quarter deck.

The larger quarter deck on to which Sir George Grey had stridden, much needed cleaning up. In the north of New Zealand, a flag staff carrying the Union Jack, had been cut down by an insurgent chief. A settlement had been sacked, with completeness and the chivalry innate in the Maoris. No hurt was done the whites, that could be avoided, nor was there looting of property. The Maoris let Bishop Selwyn wash the earth with the contents of a spirit cask. It was all sobriety in victory.

'They were,' Sir George noted of his favourite native race, ' naturally ambitious of military renown ; they were born warriors.' British troops had been hurled against their pas, or fortresses, only to be hurled back, heaps of slain. A Maori pa, in some forest fastness, stoutly built for defence from within, held by determined men with firearms, was hard to storm. Gallantry rushed to suicide.

The Maori wars, in their broad sense, are history. It is enough here to define them as the collision of two races. The white tide of civilisation was beating upon the foreshores of native New Zealand. There were King Canutes, tattooed warriors of the flying day, who would have ordered it back. You see how easily troubles grew, although they might have been the last desire of anybody.

Two Maori chieftains, Heke and Kawiti, were the centre of disturbance, and Sir George Grey was to have faithful dealing with them. Heke he called the fighting chief, Kawiti the advising chief ; one the complement of the other.

'When I met Heke after the war,' he mentioned, ' it was said that he was somewhat nervous. I thought I was the person who should have been nervous, because I was in his country almost alone. I liked him,

and really all the old Maori chiefs were fine fellows—
shrewd, dignified, with a high sense of honour. Heke
made me his heir when he died, to the neglect of his
wife, but of course I gave her everything.'

This Heke was the son-in-law of Hongi, a Na-
poleonic figure in Maori annals. Hongi was before
Sir George's time, but he heard all about him from
contemporaries.

New Zealand, when Hongi had the guidin' o't,
was still a land remote from the concern of the Old
World. Missionaries had begun to spread light in
the country; runaway convicts from Australia arrived
stealthily, seeking refuge. For the rest, Hongi and
the Maoris were the war lords, and the fiery torch
was generally abroad.

Hongi visited England, was lionised as a New
Zealand trophy, and presented, with every ceremony,
to the Prince Regent, afterwards George IV. He
got many presents, and, before reaching New Zealand
again, he exchanged them to a purpose which the givers
could hardly have foreseen. Hongi had been quick to
discern the road to conquest, which musket, gun-
powder, and bullet, would give him in New Zealand
against the native weapons. He chortled to himself
as did Lamech: 'I have slain a man to my wounding,
and a young man to my hurt.'

'Landing with his battery of muskets,' Sir George
had the tale, 'Hongi lost no time in carrying slaughter
through Maoriland. His lurid fame spread far and
wide; his bill of slaughter grew bigger and bigger.

Yet, he met his death by a stray shot. Te-Whero-Whero, another Maori chief, complained to me, while we were discussing Hongi, that it was quite unfair he should have been cut down in that fashion. When a veteran warrior could be destroyed, almost by accident, to the gun of a nobody, then all honest fighting was at an end. " You should," I was earnestly counselled by Te-Whero-Whero, " not let Maoris have arms which lend themselves to such ways." '

One English gift Hongi had not converted into muskets, a suit of armour that had probably been in the Tower of London. 'Another chief near Wellington '—Sir George stated this item arising out of Hongi—' had been given the armour, either to inspect or to keep. Anyhow, his interest took the form of hanging it on a tree, and firing at it. The bullet, it was alleged, penetrated the armour, and a native ran to Wellington with the report that the chief had been shot. That was incorrect, for he wisely wanted to test the armour before trusting himself in it. But the English settlers, just beginning to arrive in Wellington, were disturbed lest the tribe should fall foul of the representatives of a country which has produced so treacherous a suit of mail.'

Knowledge of arms, on the part of the Maoris, had advanced ; indeed, they were in no wise tardy to pit themselves against British troops. Their own success, or rather the want of success of the British, had brought about this state of feeling. Careful, direct

study of the situation, upheld Sir George in the
intuition that he must strike firmly at the rebellion,
and take every civil step that would tend to lay it.
He stopped the sale of arms to the natives, though
for another reason than that advanced by Te-Whero-
Whero. Some fancied that his action might occasion
discontent, if not revolt, among the friendly Maoris.
' Well,' was his answer, ' if that is a risk, we must
run it.'

He gripped the nettle of land dealing, as between
whites and natives, admonishing : ' The State shall
conduct it. Then, it will be seen what the Maori
has to sell, and the European will be made certain of a
proper title. We shall have a regular system, the
State standing between the parties to secure that all
is fair. Thus friction may be avoided.' Again, Sir
George organised a native police force, which paid a
double debt. It not only waited upon law and order,
but exercised a civilising influence towards the Maoris,
through those who were trained in its ranks. That
aim was at the end of all his plans ; every road was
marked ' To Civilisation.'

Next, Sir George took the field. By accompany-
ing the soldiers, he was able to gain a variety of
advantages. He was at hand to sanction what steps
might be necessary, an advance on cumbrous despatch
writing. His presence was especially valuable when
sea and land forces happened to be co-operating. He
could order both, being Governor, Commander-in-
Chief, Lord High Admiral, and everything else, in New

Zealand. Finally, he could speak, face to face, with the Maoris, friends and enemies, in the name of the Queen.

On the *Elphinstone* he had devoted his hours to the study of Maori, following his principle, ' You cannot govern a race, to the best advantage, unless you are able to communicate with them in their own language. They will receive you more intimately if you thus meet them ; they will tell you things which they would not care to confide to an interpreter. Moreover, to know the language of a people is a great assistance to the entire understanding of them, their needs and characteristics. My Maori helped me enormously, and the language, with its rich folk-lore and tradition, fascinated me as I grew in knowledge of it.'

The main stronghold of Heke and Kawiti was a pa designated, in Maori, Ruapekapeka, of which the English equivalent is 'Bat's-Nest.' Here the Maoris were in martial clover, having reasoned with themselves : 'We'll build a pa the Pakehas can't take, if we are behind its walls. We await them in this place, and if they want us, just let them come on.' That was Sir George Grey's summary of the resistance which the English forces, moving to invest Ruapekapeka, had to meet. Fortune smiled, and exacted little as return sacrifice.

'Our force,' he narrated, 'was strengthened by a detachment of friendly Maoris under the command of Waka Nene, a grizzled warrior. He was my chief adviser among the Maoris, and his services were of the utmost value to me. Waka Nene recognised the necessity, in New Zealand, of a government which could control both races. The former mistake, of trying to storm a well-defended pa, was replaced at Ruapekapeka by an artillery bombardment. Having made myself familiar with the method of warfare pursued by the Maoris, I decided this to be our line of tactics. They could use their Tower muskets with effect, but of artillery they had none, except a few old ships' guns, which they would have been better without.

' We had pounded the " Bat's-Nest " heavily, when, on a Sunday, Waka Nene's brother, Wi Waka, made out, from our front, that it seemed to be more or less empty. The Maoris had gone to a sheltered spot to celebrate divine service, thinking perhaps that Sunday was not a battle day with us. They relied upon our observing Sunday for praise and rest, unaware that Christian nations have done much of their hardest fighting on that day. Immediately we learned of Wi Waka's discovery, our men advanced into the pa. Rushing back to occupy it, at the alarm, the Maoris met us already in possession. They endeavoured, with vigour and gallantry, to drive us out, but could not, and the whole affair was over in a quarter of an hour.

' Wi Waka sustained a severe wound in the encounter, being shot through the ribs, on the left side. Hearing of this, I ran to him, and he asked me would he die of the wound or not ? I replied that I could not tell, that possibly it might not be a fatal wound, but on the other hand it might be. When I had spoken he took my hand and said, "Have I done my duty to-day? Say!"

'Several chiefs had by this time gathered round, and we were all much touched by Wi Waka's appeal. I could only answer, "Yes, certainly! You have done your duty nobly." He turned to the chiefs: "Did you hear the Governor's word? I don't care now, if I die." Happily he recovered, but the incident showed the spirit of the man, and he was an example of the others.'

The English force, Sir George made the postscript, was to have assailed the 'Bat's-Nest' on the Monday, the defences being much knocked about. The intention was to assault from the rear, and he believed they would have been certain of the enemy, without incurring any considerable loss.

The fall of Ruapekapeka brought peace to the northern half of New Zealand, and when the Governor visited Heke it was 'To explain to him that I was his friend, which he admitted.'

Some of the folks in New Zealand blamed Sir George for being too indulgent towards revolted Maoris, fearing, 'In thanks they will raid Auckland some day, and massacre us all.' A retired military officer, inclined to that view, was staying at Government House, Auckland, the night a fire destroyed it and Sir George's earliest group of literary treasures.

'When a shout went up, on the discovery of the fire,' Sir George laughed in recollection, 'my guest fancied that his prophecy about the Maoris had come true. He looked out of his bedroom window, saw Maoris about, and assured himself that an attack on us had begun. He barricaded his door with a chest of drawers, the chairs, whatever he could lay hands on. Being a man of military training he prepared for a desperate siege, and this so effectively, that I believe he had, on learning the real state of matters, to escape the fire by crawling through the window.

Afterwards, the Governor had a critic the fewer, of his olive branch to the Maoris.

X

'TWIXT NIGHT AND MORN

NIGHT and morning in the far south were vividly reflected to Sir George Grey in tales of Rauparaha and Rangihaeta, Maori chieftains, and of Siapo, Loyalty Islander.

Before his arrival in New Zealand, the Maoris had been divorced from their cannibal practices. Yet, the horrid traffic was not remote, if he were to accept a lasting rumour of Rauparaha and Rangihaeta. The pair were making their own war stir for him, and must be tackled. It was earlier that, sitting on a hillside in friendly converse, they sent a slave girl for a pail of water. As she tripped off to do their bidding, Rauparaha, the story was, shot her through the back for a meal. No doubt cannibalism, among the Maoris, had thriven on the absence of animal meat, for New Zealand was peculiar in that respect. Its one large creature of the lower world was the moa, of which Sir George said 'It was akin to the ostrich, but no European, I believe, ever saw it alive.'

Governor Grey and Bishop Selwyn were out together on a walking expedition, and it was Easter

Sunday. 'Christ has risen!' Selwyn reverently welcomed the day, and his companion joined, 'Indeed He has.' They were communing in that spirit when a bundle of letters, sent from Auckland to intercept them, was brought into the tent. One to Selwyn bore the news of the death of Siapo, who had become a Christian under his teaching, and who was being educated, with other natives, at his seminary in Auckland.

The Bishop, overcome with grief, burst into tears; then broke some moments of silence with the words, 'Why, you have not shed a single tear!'

'No,' said Sir George, 'I have been so wrapped in thought that I could not weep. I have been thinking of the prophecy that men of every race were to be assembled in the kingdom of heaven. I have tried to imagine the wonder and joy prevailing there, at the coming of Siapo, the first Christian of his race. He would be glad evidence that another people of the world, had been added to the teaching of Christ.'

'Yes, yes,' Selwyn remarked, drying his tears, 'that is the true idea to entertain, and I shall not cry any more.'

What a touching incident! It shows us the depth of feeling which united Governor and Bishop. Only Sir George's version ran, 'It illustrated Selwyn's great, good heart. Stalwart, quite the muscular Christian, he had the simple heart of the child. He was a man entirely devoted to his duty, counting nothing of trouble or reward. We worked hand in

H 2

hand. During an illness in New Zealand, I drew out a constitution, such as I believed would best suit the Church of England there. Broadly, it came into operation, and in a speech, when he was leaving New Zealand, Selwyn told of its origin.'

You seek life pictures, rather than any chronology of dates, and therefore to a second incident of Sir George and Selwyn on tramp. They were in the Taupo range of mountains, and their supply of food had run very short. By the borders of Lake Taupo they sighted the house of a Maori chief who, being absent, had shut it up. Believing he might find inside a stay to their wants, Sir George forced the door, and after that a cupboard. In it were rice and sugar and other supplies, which he exhibited to Selwyn with the triumphant shout, ' Here, I'll make you a present of all this ! '

' I'm afraid,' the Bishop gently remonstrated, ' that there will be trouble about our doings. You see we have really broken into somebody's house.'

' Oh, no,' Sir George reassured him, ' I know the chief who owns the place, and he would give us part of himself.'

On the following day they met the chief, as he was returning home at the head of a string of his men. Sir George informed him of the straits to which he and the Bishop had been put, and of what they had done, and received this approval, ' Well, that was like true friends, and I'm so glad you did it ! '

' You can realise,' Sir George drew the inference,

'how easy it was for me to get on with so chivalrous a race as the Maoris!' He and they had arrived at a mutual comprehension of each other. They recognised his parts, the manner in which he could make himself felt where least expected, the difficulty of beating him in expedients, his desire to advance their interests and happiness, his tender care for them as a father, after he had ridden as the Cæsar. Towards the full understanding, his bout with Rauparaha and Rangihaeta was, perhaps, an assistance.

'The name Rauparaha,' he narrated, 'means in Maori a cabbage leaf; a wild cabbage leaf. The tradition was that Rauparaha's father was killed and eaten by some rival chief. While eating him, the other chief mumbled with inward satisfaction, "This man eats like a young cabbage." The son, being told, vowed revenge, and took the name Rauparaha to emphasise the fact. It was insulting, he felt, to laugh over the eating of his father.'

Sir George's pledge for peace was the opening up of the country by means of roads, and he drove these hither and thither. The power of resistance which the Maoris manifested in warfare, kept anxiety simmering at Downing Street.

'In that connection,' Sir George said, 'Earl Grey, as Colonial Secretary, consulted the Duke of Wellington on the best policy for securing the durable settlement of the Maoris. The Duke, I learned from Earl Grey himself, advised the making of roads which would knit New Zealand, and employ the natives.

Just after Earl Grey had seen the Duke, he had despatches from me, in which I outlined, in almost as many words, what I had been doing.'

The coincidence struck Sir George, and it gratified him to have the Duke in agreement. He was supported by another eminent soldier, when, at a London dinner party, being asked to give his opinion of the conduct of the Crimean War, he answered, ' I should have attacked upon the St. Petersburg side, where you could really get at Russia, instead of on the Crimean side, with its strong forts, its distance from the centre of the empire, and a food supply confined to that carried by the ships.'

In New Zealand he had no difficulty in getting Maori labour, since it was fairly paid, and excellent trunk roads were the result. Rauparaha took the innovation with a seeming unconcern, meant to hide an adverse feeling, which Rangihaeta, however, frankly expressed. He could look back upon his years, old Rauparaha, and mark in them enough stir and fight to satisfy a score of warriors. Age had crawled on to his shoulders, causing his furtive eyes to rest on the ground. But he was still himself, as Sir George Grey realised, on receiving certain information. It indicated that Rauparaha was in a league of mischief, that he had quietly given a signal, and that large bodies of natives were drawing down the coast to his aid. Farther, it was put to Sir George that an attack on Wellington was the evident object. This would be calamity, for the forces available as a defence, at short notice, were small. Now for the Governor's action, which some criticised as high-handed.

'At first,' he related the exploit, 'I was doubtful whether I could fairly attribute the scheme to Rauparaha. However, I satisfied myself that the information which had reached me was well-founded. It had been brought by a man who was in touch with the Maoris creeping down the coast, and who could speak Maori. These bodies of natives, you understand, had prevented all news travelling. That was how they were able to get so near, without our being aware of it.

'What was I to do? Was I to delay until actually attacked? That would have been to wait for too much proof of the plot; and my information satisfied me. I had a picked force put on board a man-of-war lying at Wellington, and with it, and another small vessel, we set out for Rauparaha's country. Besides myself, only three or four of the officers, I suppose, knew the nature of our mission. We landed, after dark, at a point of the sea coast near Rauparaha's camp, quietly surrounded it, burst in and captured him. The thing was to swoop into the camp before the Maoris could have any warning, or attempt to resist. Thus an encounter, involving slain and wounded, would be avoided. Rauparaha was taken off to the ships in a boat, and we conveyed him to Wellington.

'The results were as I had anticipated, for Rauparaha being our prisoner, there was nobody to give the word of command to the Maori disaffectants, who melted away. I told Rauparaha there were two courses open to him. He could take his trial, before an open court, for what he had done, or he could remain a prisoner, until I thought the interests of peace would permit me to release him. He elected to continue my prisoner, and other chiefs became bail for him when I did let him go.

'Rauparaha's defence was that he intended no harm, and that he was not in the plot, for he admitted there was a plot. I asked him why, if he meant no harm, he did not tell me that all these men had come so near. To that he had no answer, and besides I submitted to him a letter, which had been sent up the coast, telling the men to march down. He called the letter a forgery, but there was no question, in my judgment, that it was dictated by him and circulated by his desire. The best proof of its genuineness was that its plan was carried out, that the Maoris did collect in response to it. Nobody could have managed the business but Rauparaha.

'What would have been the outcome of an attack on Wellington? Turmoil! I certainly believe that it would have been attacked. Then, a large force must have been sent to punish the raiders, or Wellington would have had to be abandoned. In either event, the progress of New Zealand would have been thrown back for years.'

Though restored to his tribe, Rauparaha never regained his power, and was a desolate man. It was a characteristic of the Maoris, that when a chief had a tumble he lost his influence. To that detail Sir George added another, namely that Rauparaha was a very good speaker. Indeed, many of the Maoris had the true gift of eloquence. Rauparaha left some Maori manuscripts, about himself, to the Governor who had so unceremoniously made him captive. It was a tribute to that Governor's genius for attaching the regard of men, converting even enemies into friends.

Another instance, and another incident, lie in the conversion of Rangihaeta to road-making. He had rushed to the rescue of Rauparaha, on hearing of his capture. It was the chivalrous daring of one chief, towards the brother in distress, but unavailing. Not a hair of anybody's head had been hurt, yet Rauparaha was already beyond his friend's reach. Rangihaeta sulked into his own fastnesses—a rumble of discontent and vengeance. Sir George did not wish him to remain in a state holding so little happiness. Moreover, the all-important high roads must invade even Rangihaeta's territory. Diplomatic overtures were not wasted ; they blossomed quietly, and then bloomed on an inspiration.

'When the old fellow had begun to get frail and ill,' said Sir George, 'I sent him a pretty pony and trap. The sea shore, at his part of New Zealand, offered a splendid stretch of firm sand, one of the finest drives in the world. Delighted with his carriage, he would use it ; only a breadth of rough land intervened between his pa and the beach. He could not drive across it, so what does he do but turn out his men to make a roadway.

'There was merriment in Maoriland at the idea that Rangihaeta, hitherto sternly opposed to our roads, should himself be constructing one. That was, as I had hoped, and he made no more difficulties for us. How could he? There he was, almost every afternoon, driving on the sands in all the pride of peacock feathers. Not merely that, but he aired his sister Topera, a woman of first-rate abilities, and of wide influence among the Maoris.'

Meanwhile, an outbreak at Wanganui furnished Sir George with material for his administrative wits. He was strolling up and down, deep in meditation, on a sort of terrace at his residence in Auckland. Turning, he noticed a Maori running towards him, and the next moment the Maori was rubbing his nose against the Governor's, the native fashion of salute.

Sir George, himself, had raced one of the fleetest members of a Maori tribe, throwing off his coat to do it, and proving the victor. 'I was somewhere on the coast, with several of my officers and a number of Maori chiefs, and there was a debate as to running. I ventured the statement that I could, perhaps, beat the Maoris at a distance contest. They selected their best man, a young chief, and I fancy it took me more than half a mile to get away from him.'

Those civilities were very well in their place, but the Governor would have dispensed with the nose rubbing of the native at his doorstep, so anxious was he to learn the reason. There was news in the man's face, and when he gathered words, it proved to be that of the Wanganui outbreak.

A spark there, had been the going off, by mishap, of a midshipmite's pistol. The lad was toying with it, amusing himself and a Maori chief. ' Look here, old fellow ! ' he had exclaimed, and to his own amazement the pistol went bang, hurting the chief in the face.

Extracting from his Maori mercury, every point of information he could furnish, Sir George ordained silence upon him, lest uneasiness might be caused among the people of Auckland. Then, on the plea of making a rapid tour of the outposts of the Colony, he organised a move on Wanganui. He went thither by sea, with a contingent of troops and a body-guard of leading Maori chiefs.

' These,' Sir George smiled, ' had been vowing all sorts of handsome things to me, and I took them at their word. I said to them that no better opportunity could arise, enabling them to fulfil their promises. They would be beside me, ready to send orders to their several tribes, should the assistance of these be needed. I need hardly add, that nothing untoward could happen in the localities which the chiefs denoted, while they were absent with me. Generally, I went about with a group of them in my train, as I preferred to have the possibilities of trouble with me. They took kindly to travel, and they always behaved most admirably towards me.'

As his vessel touched the Wanganui shore, a Maori

was seen scouring along it, in desperate haste. Behind, there raced a thread of enemies, Maoris on the war-path, but the man plunged into the surf before they could overtake him. Sir George imagined that here was another messenger, with information from the little Wanganui garrison of British soldiers. It was necessary he should hear tidings without a moment's delay, and he jumped into the ship's boat, which had been lowered to pick up the swimmer. The latter was pulled into it dripping wet, and in a rare state of excitement.

He seized Sir George, to salute him in Maori fashion, and the roll of the boat sent them both sprawling among the thwarts. Not minding that, the Maori kept vigorously rubbing the nose of his Excellency, who made the plaintive comment, 'I could not help myself. Besides, I had no grievance, unless that the Maori was using up, with his nose, precious minutes, to which he might better have given his tongue. That's an unusual compliment to pay the latter human member.'

The Wanganui crisis was settled by a show of strength, and a shrewd ukase, for Sir George set himself against more fighting. The recalcitrant Maoris had been accustomed to come down the river to trade, getting in return, sugar, tobacco, and other dainty necessaries.

'I shut them off from all that, until such time as they should submit, and undertake to live in peace. Neither could they meet their friends, and tiring of these laws, they gave in.' It was the boycott, employed by a Queen's servant, long before the word itself entered our language.

During the disturbances, a Maori leader, in sincere quest for tobacco, found something more deadly. He was rummaging a provision chest, not his own, when a wandering bullet plunged through the roof of the wooden cottage. It entered his head and put out his pipe for ever.

The occurrence gave the Maoris an eerie shiver, for it was as if death had fallen straight from Heaven. They were learning to look up there, though a chief, the story went, once rebuked a missionary : 'You tell me to turn my gaze to Heaven, not to care for earthly things, and all the time you are grabbing my land.'

XI

THE THRILL OF GOVERNING

NOTHING is small in the making of an empire. It is the seeming trifles that often shape the way, fair or foul.

This was a clear article of faith in Sir George Grey, and he would give it picturesque sittings. It had been with him wherever he carried the flag; it dotted Australia, New Zealand, and South Africa with milestones of policy. These might not be visible to others, but he knew, having planted them. They told of what had been done, by means of the little things; a bulwark against the undoing of the great things. Ever, the handling of personal elements was the master touch, the vast secret.

Take Sir George's entrance into the circle of Knights Commanders of the Bath, with Waka Nene and Te Puni for Esquires. He was one of the youngest K.C.B.s ever nominated, being only thirty-six, and he just preceded his old friend Sir James Stephen. 'It struck me as a great shame,' his feeling had been, 'that one to whom I was so much attached, whose services to the State were so much longer than mine, should be made to follow me in the "Gazette." I could have cried over it.'

The notion of Esquires belongs, no doubt, to the truculent age when a brace of henchmen were useful beside the stirrup of a knight. Sir George did not revive them, in New Zealand, as a body-guard in any warlike meaning. Herein, there possibly lay a certain disappointment for his friends Waka Nene and Te Puni, both Maori chiefs of martial qualities. The purpose was to identify the Maori people with a reward, which the Queen of England had conferred upon her representative in New Zealand.

'It is not for me alone,' Sir George Grey put the honour, 'but for all of us in this distant part of the realm. Therefore you, Waka Nene and Te Puni, shall join in the acceptance, in proof that the Queen forgets none of her subjects, no matter who they may be, or where they may dwell.'

This was a sprig of the policy which he felt must be pursued by an Empire called to boundless limits. Did it rest its control of the nations, successively adopted into it, upon their fears, upon a compelled obedience ? Why, it would but grow the weaker as it spread, until eventually a time must arrive when, from its very vastness, it would fall into fragments. On the other hand, if, as it spread its dominion, it also spread equal laws, the Christian faith, Christian knowledge, and Christian virtues, it would link firmly to itself, by the ties of love and gratitude, each nation it adopted. Thus, it would grow in strength as it grew in area, its dominion being an object sought for, rather than submitted to impatiently.

Go into the engine-room of administration, and listen to the clatter of yon modest pinion in a corner ! That is, follow the avoidance of a peril in New Zealand, which might easily have sown more seeds of race warfare. There had been a mysterious, deadly tragedy on the outskirts of Auckland, a retired naval lieutenant and his family the victims. The affair profoundly moved the young community, having regard to the unrest which had been rife in the land. Several natives were arrested as suspects, and Europeans put it to the Governor, 'We shall certainly all be murdered, unless you deal sharply with them.'

A leading Maori chief of the district went away, to be out of the serious trouble which, he feared, might arise at any moment. The Governor sent after him the message : 'The manner in which to meet difficulty is not to flee from it, and you must come back. I relied upon you to behave with sense and courage, and I'm confident you will still bear me out in that view.' The chief did return, but said Sir George, ' He upbraided me as being, to all appearance, a Governor quite unable to deal with such a problem as confronted me.' This was an exquisite turning of the tables.

'Why,' argued the old Maori, ' could you not at once have hanged the natives who were arrested ? If you had done that, everybody's mind would have been at rest, but, as things are, nobody feels safe. We imagine that we may be blamed for the crime, while the English can have no confidence so long as no person has been punished. You see at what we have arrived.'

Any spark might now fire the bracken, and it was the task of Sir George to prevent that. His despatches and blue-books, fodder for the browse of Downing Street, had to wait upon this other business, which would not even go into them. Not unless there was a crash, during a moment's want of vigilance, or by lack of perfectly deft management. The greater empire making, it is evident, was not to have to write any blue-books. None were written, for the tension between European and Maori, healed in the hands of the patient doctor. It turned out that a Van Diemen's Land convict was the villain of that remote new Zealand drama.

Patoune, an influential Maori chief, had been zealous in the unfathoming of the mystery, and mentioning that, Sir George Grey was led to say, 'Some time before his death Patoune rowed over from Auckland to my island at Kawau. Seeing the boat coming, I walked down to the shore to meet its occupant and conduct him indoors, where we had a long conversation. On leaving he spoke, " Yes, I wanted to be with you once more, before I go the way of all men. I have had my last fallen-out tooth set in a walking-stick, which pray accept, a mark of our friendship." As you can suppose, this affected me deeply. A piece of bone is a kind of Maori talisman, and Patoune meant his tooth to bring luck to me.

He thought my carrying it about with me, might one day save me from misfortune.'

The incidents of governing are incongruous ; they jostle queerly. An official letter was put into the hands of Sir George Grey, as he stood on the sea-shore at Wanganui, watching a skirmish in progress with the Maoris. He seated himself, opened the envelope, and forgot the crack of muskets in the document it contained. This was a first constitution for New Zealand, and he was instructed to introduce the same. He didn't ; only that is a very red-letter tale. It should be told simply, as Sir George Grey told it.

'In the middle of the turmoil at Wanganui,' he stated, 'out comes a constitution which had been passed by the British Parliament, and published in the "Gazette." It was, you understand, to be the instrument under which the New Zealand people should take their full, free place in the Empire. Up to that date they had not been self-governing ; the Governor ruled. Well, having studied it carefully where I sat, I arrived at the conclusion that it would not do at all.

'Conceive my surroundings ! There I was, with Maori chiefs whom I had brought from Auckland and Wellington. They trusted me ; they were helping me all they could to bring about a peace. This constitution, I discovered, would destroy, at one stroke, a treaty—that of Waitangi, which every Maori in New Zealand held to be sacred. It was a treaty securing them in their lands; it was their Magna Charta in every respect. Yet the constitution would go back upon all that, and I should be held traitor to every one of my pledges to the Maoris. Moreover, it would have seemed as if I had taken the chiefs away from their various tribes, in order that these might be the more readily despoiled of their lands.

'Its treatment of the Maoris made the constitution impossible, in my judgment, and there were other far-reaching objections. It was formed on the cast-iron methods of the Old World—the methods which, I held, ought to be kept absolutely out of the New World. My motto might have been, "Leave us to ourselves; let us try what we can contrive." What was I to do with a constitution unjust to the bulk of the colonists, as well as to the Maoris; a plan going tilt against the federation idea which I hoped would, in future years, uprise in every country speaking the English tongue?

'What was I to do indeed? My instruction was not alone that of the Colonial Office; but the constitution had been sanctioned by Parliament. A man's responsibility, in the largest sense, is, after adequate deliberation, to proceed as he determines to be just and wise. If he has to decide, not for himself only, but for others, unto future generations, there lies his course all the more. There was one clear line for me, simply to hang up the constitution, and intimate to the home authorities my ideas about it. This I did, and fortunately, as I thought, my plea prevailed with the Colonial Secretary and with Parliament. The latter not merely went back upon its act, a quite extraordinary event in English Parliamentary history, but empowered me to draw up another constitution for New Zealand.'

You seek, for a moment, to contemplate the Mother of Parliaments having a measure she had given forth, bluntly returned upon her. It was a trying experience, but she emerged from it more worthy than ever of her proud title. 'We shall give him,' Peel declared, when Sir George Grey went to New Zealand, 'an assurance of entire confidence. We shall entrust to him, so far as is consistent with the constitution and laws of this country, an unfettered discretion.' Parliament lived up to that promise, and Sir George set himself to the mapping out of an adequate constitution.

'The circumstances under which I drafted it,' he resumed his account, 'were peculiar, not to say romantic. The folks in New Zealand were aware of the work that had been delegated to me, and of the date at which it must be carried out. I was to have the constitution going within five years. There were various interests, and some of these would advance the request, "Tell us what you are to recommend ; let us have a part in framing the laws under which we are to be governed. You are an autocrat in your ways, and it is intolerable that we should not have a voice in the matter."

'Then I consulted my Executive Council, and I

found it the autocrat, unwilling to let me do anything
at all. I believed that, if left to myself, I could
fashion something which would secure the gratitude
of New Zealand for all time. I fancied I was capable
of that ; as I had visions of a new form of constitution
being helpful, far beyond New Zealand. In the end,
when my thoughts had bent to a shape, I went up
into the mountains between Auckland and Wellington, camped on Ruapehu, in a little gipsy tent, and
set to the task. A few Maoris accompanied me to
carry the baggage ; nobody else, for I could not
have drawn the constitution with a cloud of advisers
about me.

'Where did I get my inspiration ? Oh, by talking
to the hills and trees, from long walks, and many
hints from the United States constitution. I sought
a scheme of government which should be broad, free,
charged with a young nation's vitality. But the
greatest merit of my constitution, was that the people
of New Zealand could alter it at any point, should
they desire to do so. That was why it appeared to
me unnecessary to ask a number of leading men :
Did they approve what I was doing ? I aimed at a
most liberal constitution, and they could change it to
their wishes as time went on.'

Sir George held man's highest education to be
that, which taught him the rights and duties of
citizenship. No call could be more noble ; indeed
here was the essence of all service and religion.
Therefore, he conceived the best system of govern-

ment, to be one wherein the opportunities for the exercise of citizenship were the fullest. What could be more pathetic than the cramping of aspirations, such as had been seen in the case of Ireland ? It was as if the roots of a tree were half destroyed, so preventing the full flow of strength into the trunk.

Sir George Grey's New Zealand constitution was thus inspired. There was in it the breath of the mountains, to which he had gone, as the great law-giver of the Jews went up into them to pray. It proclaimed a minute self-government, ending in a central Parliament. The powers in London approved it, with a modification which, looking backward, he pronounced a vital wound. He made both the Houses of Parliament elective ; the modification made one nominative. It spoiled the fabric of his handiwork.

'The kernel of my plan,' he said, 'was a form of complete home rule, denominated in provinces. My idea was to give all the localities the right to levy their own taxes, and establish their own immediate rules. The great landowners were always antagonistic to this, believing that these councils would tax them, when a single Parliament, by the influence they might assert upon it, especially through a nominated Upper House, would not do so. Such was the force which, twenty years later, led to the destruction of the New Zealand Provincial Councils.'

The old war-horse was not neighing for the fray, that being all over ; he was just putting his foot-note to a piece of history he had fashioned. It suggested another. The Duke of Newcastle was concerned in the drawing up of the Canadian constitution. He informed the author of the New Zealand one, that he had been largely indebted to it. Mention of the Duke brought a smile on Sir George's lips, but he had doubts whether he should divulge the cause.

'You know,' the reminiscence ran, 'I used, when in England, to visit the Duke of Newcastle at Clumber. I was there, a member of a party, on a wet day when we were cooped up in the house, unable to find occupation. Towards afternoon, everybody being in despair, I proposed, "Why not have some cock-fighting?" Not the illegal cock-fighting of course, but the nursery-room style, where you have your hands tied in front of your knees, and try to turn an opponent over with your toes. My proposal was received with delight, and I suppose half a dozen of the leading men of England, were that afternoon kicking their heels in the air.'

Sir George could catch laughter, when a burden really did rest upon his acts—catch it, to carry the burden away. The quaint instance of how he got the better of the Maori children of Poa was in point. A member of that New Zealand tribe had come under the weights of justice at Auckland. The clansmen mustered to his rescue, and were willed to turn Auckland upside down, if necessary, in achieving it. The Governor heard betimes of the advance of their war canoes, and he arranged his welcome.

'I called out our defensive forces, including a

corps of pensioners settled in the locality, and placed them in position round the bight, where I supposed the Maoris would land. A man-of-war, which was in the harbour, I sent out to sea, with instructions to return when the invaders had arrived, and to block their exit. But everything was as if there had been nothing ; not a sign that we expected callers with hostile intent.

'The Maoris rowed to the landing with vigour and confidence, forming indeed a picturesque sight, though I was little inclined to dwell on that at the moment. Next, they began to drag their canoes ashore ; but here a signal was given, and our half-circle of troops revealed themselves. The Ngatipoa evidently did not know what to make of the changed situation, or what to do. I sat on a hill and watched them, waiting for a move on their part, which presently came. It was no business of mine to do more than I had done ; let them now propose ? They sent up their leader, escorted by a few men, to ask what I meant to do in the circumstances. That was considerate.

'I had already agreed with myself that the thing was, by hook or crook, to get rid of the Ngatipoa in a peaceable fashion. To make prisoners of them all was not possible, even had it been wisdom ; the others might have done mischief. There were friends of my own among the Maoris, and I relied upon them as an assistance towards a solution. I must make the vaunted Ngatipoa in a measure ridiculous ; treat them

as if they were naughty children. I addressed the
chief, " How could you be so foolish ? I had thought
you a wise fellow." He did not say what he thought
I was, but admitted frankly the object of the raid. He
asked me to allow them to leave quietly, and I consented, on condition they went at once.

'They petitioned to remain until the tide was at
the flow, when they could readily get their big canoes
afloat. But I was firm, fearing that if they lingered
they might mix with the townspeople, be chaffed, and
retaliate. Besides, I was determined that they should,
as a lesson in humility, have the labour and indignity
of pulling their canoes over the shingle. It vexed
them sore, after having arrived with a war-whoop, to
be obliged to beat so menial a retreat. However,
they must submit to the toil and the jeers they had
laid up for themselves, by their behaviour. As they
were exhausted, I granted them leave to remain for
the night at a pa, some miles distant from Auckland.
Next day they forwarded me a penitent letter, through
Selwyn, if I remember aright.

'The folks of Auckland had all turned out to
witness the sport, and were very proud of the successful result. They were convinced, most of them,
that they had something to do with bringing it
about. A picture of the scene was painted to com-
memorate it. What worried me, was that I was
made to look so young beside my officers—younger
really than I was. Earlier, Peel had said of me, on
the same text, that youth ought to be no bar to public

employment, and that, anyhow, it was a fault which was always mending.'

Sir George Grey had established New Zealand with peace, and an ever rising prosperity. The two fondled these isles, as the Pacific Ocean lapped their shores.

'On your arrival,' wrote the Maoris in one of their many farewell addresses to him, 'the rain was beating, and the wind blowing fiercely ; and then you lifted up your voice to calm the raging elements.'

England needed his spell elsewhere.

XII

IN THE QUEEN'S NAME

THE example of one gallant-minded, stout cadet, was maybe with Carlyle when he pictured the Queen in Council to pick out some other, still unoccupied, and adjure him in royal words :

'Young fellow, if there do be in you potentialities of governing, a gradual finding, leading, and coercing to a noble goal, how sad it is that that should be all lost. I have scores on scores of colonies. One of these you shall have. Go and grapple with it in the name of Heaven, and let us see what you will build of it.'

To Carlyle Sir George Grey might have gone, and laid at his feet South Australia and New Zealand. He had been their fairy autocrat during fourteen years ; and the rugged out-looker at Chelsea would have admitted them to be healthy brats. New Zealand having been fitted with her Parliament, Sir George turned his face homeward, on leave of absence, Selwyn a fellow voyager. Mother's boy and mother hoped to meet once more, but it was not to be. The Mother-land had kept the servant too long on duty, but he grudged her not even that.

'My mother,' said Sir George softly, 'had been in frail health for some time, and I was always hoping to get home on her account. She heard that our ship had been signalled in the English Channel, then that I had landed, and she waited my appearance with loving expectation. My young step-brother entered her room, and mistaking him for me, she grasped his hand in thankfulness. The thing excited her, so very weak was she, and her death took place before I could reach her. Happily, I had at least the consolation that she believed she had seen me.'

The danger spot, in our over-sea territory, was now South Africa, where British and Dutch were at odds with each other, and both at odds with the natives. Affairs were a chaos. The region, grown historic as the Transvaal, had been told to arrange its future as it would. The Orange Free State had been kicked outside the British line of empire, with a solatium in money, in the manner that an angry father bids adieu to a ne'er-do-well son. A white man in South Africa hardly knew what flag he was living under, or, indeed, if he could claim any. Panda, on the Zululand frontier, growled over his assegai and knobkerry. Moshesh, the Basuto, hung grimly on the face of Thaba Bosego, a Mountain of Night in very truth. The embers of a Kaffir war still glowed.

Who was to hold the arena? Its hazards were thrown to Sir George Grey. At the moment, he would, perhaps, rather have returned to New Zealand, but he was told that somebody with the necessary qualifications must hie to the Cape, and that the Government had selected him. He packed his baggage and sailed from Bristol, Sir James Stephen going down there to see him embark. Bristol, as he explained, was then endeavouring to establish relations with the Cape and Australasia, which were coming into note.

'When I reached Cape Town,' Sir George pursued, 'they had just got their first Parliament, but it was hardly in operation. Under the constitution that had been granted, the Governor remained, to all purposes, the paramount force in the country. His ministers had practically no power over him, and thus everything was more or less in his hands. On urging them, as I often did, to go in for a system under which the ministers should be directly responsible to the people, not to the Governor, I would be told, " Oh, we can always get rid of you, if you do anything wrong, by an appeal to the Colonial Office." It was not until after I left the Cape that popular government was brought into effect.

'What sort of South Africa did I find? The bulk of the whites were Boers, who were most conservative in their ideas. There were no railways, and I had great difficulty in making that innovation acceptable to the Boers. Effort was requisite for the construction of harbours, a matter of equally vital importance, which I took in hand. It was desirable to give South Africa every possible element of a high civilisation, as, farther, universities, schools, and libraries. A mixture of Saxon and Dutch, she had to work out her destiny

on her own lines, untrammelled by the Old World.
Also, she must enlighten that cloud of a barbarous
Africa which was pressing down from the north.

'How South Africa has changed since then ! To
illustrate that, Bloemfontein was quite a small place in
the far wilds. Nobody knew where the capital of the
freshly created Orange Free State was to be. No
wonder either, since, for a while, many of the people
refused to accept the new form of government, and
would not vote for a President. They were angry, at
having been thrust forth from their heritage as British
subjects. What nation, they demanded, had the
right so to treat a section of its people, who had done
nothing to disqualify themselves from citizenship ?

'You have to remember that the movement for
throwing over the Colonies, was rising as an active
force in England. They had come into being almost
unbidden ; they were regarded with a cold interest.
The notion that it would be a good thing to lop them
off altogether, was being accepted among English
statesmen. You could feel the heresy in the air—
gusts that brushed your face like a chill.'

The South Africa thus put foot upon by Sir
George Grey, was re-created to him long after, in a
cablegram that he received in New Zealand. The
South African railway system, which he tended in its
infancy, had crawled north to Bloemfontein, as it has
since gone farther, and still goes on, the iron-shod
tramp. That auspicious day, Bloemfontein remembered
the author of its Grey College, and gripped his hand

across the sea. It made him very happy. Providence had set him to garden three countries of the Southern Hemisphere in rapid succession. That 'God bless you' from Bloemfontein, showed, perhaps, that he had not tilled in vain.

'There can be no harm,' said Sir George, 'in relating another incident, which kept up the kindly link between the Orange Free State and myself. Before my friend Mr. Reitz accepted its Presidency, he wrote and asked me would I be willing to consider the offer, provided it were made to me ? I was then, I think, in the quiet of Kawau Island, and I suppose Mr. Reitz believed I might be more actively employed.

'One did not need to be already a burgher of the Free State, for President Brand had not been ; at all events, that was not an obstacle. I did not see my way to regard the offer, but the making of it manifested a beautiful trait in Mr. Reitz's character. How many men, being tendered the highest post that their country could confer, would have turned to another, asking, "Will you accept it ?"'

The manner in which Sir George tackled the South African embroilment, appears in his treatment of that mongrel race, the Hottentots. They recruited largely to the Queen's Colonial service, but had a grievance in that, on leaving, they did not get, as they had been led to expect, the pension of white troopers. The 'Totties,' so christened in the Colony, might be loyal and brave, but they were not whites, and anything was good enough for them, if only it meant an Imperial saving. The Governor determined, 'This must be wiped out; its effect has already been disastrous; the Queen's uniform has but one colour.' He applied to Downing Street, only to be informed that it was not possible to reward native troopers, on retirement, as whites were. This did not content him.

'I went to the Cape Parliament, which, recognising the simple justice of my proposal, adopted it with a wise liberality. There was immediate satisfaction among the Hottentots, and on no subsequent occasion did they give trouble. It was ever my endeavour to bind the natives to us by esteem, to convince them that British rule was the most desirable rule they could have.'

How winsomely Sir George made the Queen a living personality as well as a mighty name to the native races! 'Ha-ha!' cried Maori, African, Australian, 'the Queen is indeed our mother, for Governor Grey shows it by his acts.' But the eloquent word on that, came from an old Kaffir woman, whom nobody owned, Lot Hrayi. This was her epistle, through the Governor to the Queen:

'I am very thankful to you, dearest Queen Victoria, that you have sent, for me, a good doctor, a clever man. I was sixteen years blind, Mother and Queen, but now I see perfectly. I see everything. I can see the stars, and the moon and the sun. I used to be led before; but now, Mother, O Queen, I am able to walk myself. Let God bless you as long as you live on earth; let God bless Mother! Thou must not be tired to bear our infirmities, O Queen Victoria.'

To Sir George, Lot Hrayi's dispatch was a State paper.

'Native races,' he laid down, ' understood personal rule, and the great thing was to make the Queen vivid, a reality, to them. England? Yes, it was a place far distant, where there were no dark-skinned peoples. The Queen of England? Ah, yes, they could comprehend her! She sat on a throne, so beautiful that its place must be where all was beautiful and good. Her heart beat for her folk, irrespective of their colour; she would minister to their happiness. Nothing could more delight her, than to secure the well-being of those who claimed her powerful protection. That was intelligible!

'Thus, when I had a measure of mercy, of justice, or of guidance to announce, I did it directly, in the Queen's name, and in the native languages. It was the Queen's utterance, though spoken by me, and it would be difficult to indicate how well the charm worked. Go into a cottage, in almost any part of England, and you will, I judge, find a portrait of the Queen hanging on the whitewashed walls. There were no portraits in the Kaffir kraals, yet the Queen entered them, a beneficent influence in many a crisis.'

Striving to attach the Kaffirs, Sir George granted them written titles to their lands. They could not at first perceive the object of the parchment, and he would express it thus : 'If you have any trouble with your lands, it is only necessary for you to go to a judge with this document. He will read it, and if there is a real grievance, he will have it put right. Even the Queen's army might be ordered away from a place, by a few policemen, if a judge so directed.'

The chiefs would often say afterwards : 'Oh, Sir George Grey explained to us, all about the advantages under which we held the land. He told us that the Queen, herself, could not turn us off the ground, without going to the supreme courts which dispensed justice in her name. If a claimant were found not entitled to a piece of land, he would be removed by the Queen's officers. But if he had right behind his claim, why, he would be maintained in it by those officers.'

'Some people,' Sir George made comment, 'declared it absurd that I should instil those ideas into the minds of the natives, but, in reality, it resulted in their having far more respect and regard for the Queen.' Assuredly, his policy made the Kaffirs eager to get land titles, and these were always another link binding them to good behaviour. It was the con-trivance of the silken thread, wound here, there, everywhere, as against the other method, of a horse-hair halter.

Should some swashbuckler have contrary views on native administration, he could relieve his fierceness by tracing the word 'Hottentot' to its origin. Sir

George had an amusing story of Cape Town in
controversy on this term, which the Hottentots had
always insisted did not belong to their forefathers.

'With a desire to solve the problem,' he related,
'I suggested that people in Cape Town should be
asked to write papers on the name. This proposal
was carried out, and a small sheaf of essays came in
response. Well, I was looking over an old Dutch
dictionary, and there I found " Hottentot " described
as meaning "Not speaking well; a stammerer."
The name, apparently, had been conferred by the
early Dutch settlers, in South Africa, upon the natives
first met, on account of the stuttering noise these
caused in speaking. All the competitors wanted to
have their papers back, in order, as they pleaded, to
make a few corrections.'

Again, that was a process which Sir George was
ever willing to apply to himself. Yet, being very
human, he loved to make the corrections in his own
fashion, like the essay-writers at Cape Town. There,
at the foot of Africa, he sat, bold and cautious, leading
the What-Was onward to the What-Ought-To-Be.
He might be compared to a charioteer driving two
horses, one white in two shades, jibbish at a corner,
the other black as Satan, unbroken to the bit. But
the chariot must move forward steadily, evenly, to its
greater glory.

Kaffraria had to be put on a peace footing. The
ideas, at the root of the tribal system, were averse to
the growth of civilisation, but instead of pruning

these violently, and so causing friction, Sir George would adapt them. The chiefs were largely dependent for their wealth in cattle and other chattels, on the punishments which they meted out to the tribesmen for offences, or imaginary offences. Let a Kaffir prosper, and he was certain to be charged with witchcraft. That was sudden death, and the cattle went to the kraals of him who ordered it.

The chiefs had every incentive to create witchcraft cases, thus keeping the land dark. Sir George met that, and farther bonded them fiefs of the Queen, by giving them small salaries as magistrates. He established regular courts, and in these the chiefs had their seats and a white man's guidance, while the fines went to the Government. A scarred warrior exchanged his dripping assegai for the Queen's commission as a J.P. He swaggered mightily at his bargain.

'It had,' Sir George brought up an apt anecdote, 'been promised the natives that their laws and customs should not be interfered with. After I introduced the courts, a chief was discovered to have put one of his tribe to death for witchcraft. I had the affair gone into, whereupon the chief contended, "You are aware of the undertaking we got, and trial for witchcraft is part of our customs."

'He fancied there could be no answer to this, and the other chiefs within hearing grinned approval. "Very well," I addressed him, "let us take it that way. But as you have killed this man you must support his widow. That has nothing to do with any question of custom."

'All the chiefs rolled on the ground, splitting with laughter. Knowing the penalty they might incur, the heads of tribes henceforth thought twice, before sending any man to death on a charge of witchcraft. They knew I had the means of compelling them to maintain the widow and family. I could stop the necessary amount out of their salaries. It was cheaper, and more effective, to give a bonus to a native chief than to keep a large standing army in Kaffraria.'

Sir George had worn the red coat, but he was never anxious to have it picturesquely dotting a country-side, when other measures were possible. He had bartered with Downing Street for the allowance to his chiefs. Paring down on a Budget, Disraeli bethought himself of saving half of the grant for Kaffraria. Sir George Grey entered protest. He was answered, that when difficulties had to be met at home, sacrifices must be made in the Colonies.

From tribulation, Sir George built authority. 'The fact that I was fighting the battle of the chiefs with the Home Government, naturally increased my prestige among them. They saw that I was sincere in all I had done, and that I accepted them absolutely as good friends and loyal subjects of the Queen.'

What happened? From his private means, Sir George made up, to the full amount, the instalment of salaries next due. It was a stroke which he had to repeat on a larger scale.

England raised a German legion for service in the Crimea, and, the war over, did not know what to do with the men. It was not considered wise to let them loose in England, and if they went back to Germany they might have to face the music of a drumhead court-martial. Cape Colony agreed to receive the Germans as military settlers; they would be planted, a row of defence, along the borders of Kaffraria. But the condition was attached that German families, into which the men might marry, should also be sent out.

When asked to perform the second part of the bargain, Downing Street said, 'Yes, we should like very much to do so, but we can't, for Parliament won't grant the money.'

This left the matter in an unfortunate state altogether. The German firm, managing the emigration of the families, reported to Sir George, 'The scheme must fall through, unless we have twenty thousand pounds at once.'

'I was in London,' Sir George mentioned, 'at the break between my two Governorships of South Africa. I went carefully into the matter, realising all that was at stake, and I gave the assurance, "You shall have the money this afternoon." I had never raised a large amount before, but I concluded that the place to go to was the City of London. I had several thousands with my bankers, on which I could lay hands, and I supposed they would enable me, by some method of interest, to get the remainder.

'On the road to the City I met a connexion of mine, also a banker. He asked me what I was about, and I told him. "Why don't you come to us?" he said. "I have no money with you," I replied; "and never had." "No," was his response; "but you need not pass us by in this matter. I should like to help you; come and draw a cheque for twenty thousand pounds."'

That cheque was drawn, and South Africa extracted from a grave social difficulty. The emigrants became an admirable settlement, and most honourably made good the outlay which they had occasioned.

'It wasn't banking, it wasn't business, that cheque,' Sir George was bantered long years after; 'but perhaps it was better.'

'Ah!' he laughed back, 'I'm benefiting myself now, for it seems that I returned thirty-eight shillings more than was due, and that therefore I have a balance to draw upon.'

XIII

OCEANA AND A PROPHETESS ·

SIR GEORGE GREY rode hard and far over the South African karoo, serving the Queen's writ in letters of gold. When he rode late, and the stars were ablaze, his saddle held a dreamer in dreamland.

What a lightsome new world! The sun had bathed it in the day; night brought another radiance. Here was the emblem of all the New World should be to the Old. Not yet, perhaps, in the full, for there were things to do, but soon, when the outposts of empire, stretching to Australia, New Zealand, and beyond, had come into their own. Yes, those glorious stars overhead were only meant to shine on a New World reflecting their brightness!

One winked, and Sir George smiled. Sir John Herschel had visited the Cape to fix the southern stars. The recollection carried Sir George Grey to the astronomer's part in quite a different affair. He had the tale from Herschel himself, and classed it with the somewhat relative incidents of Carlyle and Babbage. It was worse for the victim.

'Nevertheless,' said Sir George, 'his statement of it to me, was marked by much humour and enjoyment. It was the third example of my great men coming to grief through their tailor; anyhow, there lay a contributory cause. One might have moralised to Herschel on the subject of genius and clothes; I did better, I sympathised.

'Sir John, who was living near Windsor, had been up in London, and was to return home for dinner. It occurred to him that he might call, somewhere in town, about certain magnetic instruments that were being made for him, and still reach Windsor by the dinner hour. So he set off to the place, carrying in his hand certain small parcels, the contents of which were probably intended for the dinner. Remembering his quaint figure, I confess I would have given something to see him scudding along the London streets on that occasion.

'Well, when he had accomplished a good part of the journey he asked himself, "Can I do it after all?" He took out his watch, in order to ascertain what time was left him. He found that the way had occupied him longer than he had calculated; in fact, it was clearly impossible that he could go on to the instrument-maker, and also get home for dinner. He had a small party of guests that evening, and thus his punctual arrival was imperative. Having considered the dilemma for a minute, he wheeled about, satisfied that he must give up his mission if he would not spoil the dinner party. He started back in a great hurry, and at once the cry was raised, "Stop thief ! Stop thief !"

'It appeared that a policeman, full of suspicion, had been watching the not very fashionable bearer of the parcels. When Sir John came to his sudden halt, this fellow reasoned, "Ah ! he observes me ; my suspicions are confirmed." There could be no manner of doubt, on Sir John setting to run in the opposite direction. The policeman shouted, "Stop thief !" and rushed after the astronomer, a tail of curious people gathering from all sides. Sir John jogged on, heedless of the noise, ignorant of its cause, until the policeman brought him up. What was the matter ? The man of the law looked awful things, and kept a stern eye upon his prisoner, for that was now Sir John's position.

'He explained that he was hurrying home for dinner, that his wife and friends would be waiting him, and that to be detained in such fashion was a trifle absurd, especially as he was Sir John Herschel. "Sir John Herschel !" quoth the policeman ; "that's your game, is it ? No, no, my friend ; you'll have to come to the police-station with me." And away he marched the most eminent astronomer of many a year.

'At the station Sir John could only protest his identity anew, and that his account of the parcels was correct. The officials, secure in their man, commended him on his report of himself, which, they joked, was capital. Sir John Herschel ! A brilliant idea ! In the end Sir John had to send for friends who could vouch for him, and who were amazed at his plight. With many expressions of regret for the blunder, the police then allowed him to depart. He was late, to be sure, for dinner, but the worst of it was that he had no excuse to offer ; at all events he had none which he cared, then and there, to communicate to his wife and guests.'

Nobody likes to be haled before the world at a disadvantage, as Sir John Herschel was in the above experience. People, great and small, naturally wish to appear fairly in the sight of others. Anything else, were to count out a human instinct which Sir George Grey utilised, when he visited the Kaffir chief Sandilli. Sir George discovered the innocent ways, by which the kingdom of civilisation could be advanced, to be a surprising number. Moreover, they were the most effective.

Sandilli was a chief of wide influence, and as yet had not quite taken to the new order of native administration. When the Governor walked into his kraal, a full-rigged dance was in progress. Sandilli himself was leading it, and he stopped for a minute in order to welcome the visitor. 'Then he went on, more merrily than ever,' Sir George described, 'in order that I might witness how well he could dance. He wished to impress me, to show me that here was a chief, strong, agile, graceful, a Kaffir of true kingly parts. The natives were grouped in a great circle, and the ground almost shook while they danced. They sang as they leapt about, and what they sang was, "It burns ! It burns ! It burns !"

until you could almost feel the glow of fire about you. They were, in imagination, burning the kraals of some other tribe with whom they had a quarrel. "It burns ! It burns ! It burns !" I can hear them still, and realise how easily, in such a condition, they could have been led to do anything. It was fanaticism a-brew.'

The dance over, there followed business with Sandilli. He made certain requests, with which the Governor was not able to agree. It was necessary to reserve them, but this must be done in such manner that Sandilli would not be offended.

'You know,' Sir George enjoined him, 'that a child born into the world is long before it can distinguish its parents from other persons, and longer still before it can distinguish friends from foes. As yet, I am almost a new-born child in this country, and can answer no matter hurriedly. Hence, let all affairs be submitted to me in writing, and no mistakes can possibly arise.'

Sandilli and his headmen were disappointed, for they liked quick results in their diplomacy. Noting this, the Governor whipped the talk to thoughts agreeable to them. He carried them off in a happy flight, and their faces changed from gloom to mirth. When he had ridden from the kraal, and they could reflect, it was perhaps in the sense, 'We cannot quarrel with that Governor whatever may happen. He gives us no chance, but, on the contrary, entertains us.'

While Sir George Grey was King of the Cape, Moselekatsi was King of the Matabele, and the two exchanged greetings and gifts. ' Moselekatsi,' Sir George remarked, ' had left the Zulus, and set up a new nation. We never met personally, but we were on very good terms. In those days there was a great hunter in South Africa, an Englishman who had come from India, and he presented Moselekatsi with a coveted uniform. It was of the old-fashioned kind, with bulky epaulettes on the shoulders ; and what must Moselekatsi do, but remove them from there and add them to the tails ! A humorous picture he must have made, in his distorted white man's finery.'

In South Africa Sir George had the companionship of Colenso, as in New Zealand he had that of Selwyn. He likened them to each other, in their simple sincerity of nature, in their devotion to the ministry, and in their elevated ideals. They dined with those they were upbringing in the Christian faith, sitting at the head of the table, and they were complete shepherds of the flock. As Selwyn had been a walker, Colenso was a horseman, making a handsome figure in the saddle. He and Sir George would cover many a mile of veldt, eager in talk upon a Scriptural subject. It was thus when they first met, that being under the roof of Samuel Wilberforce, the famed Bishop of Oxford.

Sir George had a hunting incident of Wilberforce. On one occasion he was having a gallop with him across the green English country. Turning a corner, they met a pack of hounds, which had lost the scent and were trying to recover it.

Said Wilberforce to Sir George, 'As a bishop I have no business to go into the field, but my two boys have just donned red coats to-day, and I want to see them very much. You must, therefore, lead ·me into the field, not to follow the fox, but that I may note my boys among the company.'

It may have been in return for this service, that Wilberforce handed on to Sir George a vaunted cure for sleeplessness. The Bishop suffered, now and then, from that canker of a busy life, and some person offered to send him a sure remedy, on receipt of one sovereign, no more. Wilberforce invested, not expecting to get much, and in that not being disappointed.

'He was instructed,' Sir George bore witness, 'to imagine a flock of sheep making for a gap in a wall. Then, as he lay sleepless on his pillow, he was to watch the leader jump the gap, and count the other sheep, one by one, as they followed. The undertaking was that before the last sheep had cleared the gap, sleep should woo him. Nothing new, you see !

' But, having paid his sovereign the Bishop fancied that he might try the notion, and he did so. He confessed, with amusement, that the remedy had not done him any good, and enjoined that I might experiment without pre-payment. To carry on the fun I did this, and upon my word I think the remedy helped me once or twice. It was rather unfair to the

Bishop that I should reap the harvest of his sovereign.'

There were to be sleepless nights for Sir George,
arising from an event which he believed to be unique
in history. Some of the Kaffir chiefs, especially the
older ones, saw a danger signal in the lamp of native
progress. To them, it denoted the rising power of the
white, before whom all black men would be driven
out. These fears were magnetised into a great up-
heaval, at the word of a young Kaffir girl turned
prophetess. She uprose, a dark but comely Maid of
Orleans, a Messiah to her people, and her message
swept Kaffraria like a wind.

As any maiden might have done, Nongkause
went to fetch a pitcher of water. Most maidens,
when they filled the pitcher, would have seen the
shadow of a sweetheart in the eddies. Nongkause
saw more. Strange beings, such as were not then in
Kaffraria, were about her, and strange sounds fell upon
her ears. The remote ancestors of the Kaffirs were
revealing themselves ; their spirits were consulting on
the affairs of men.

Nongkause hurried to tell her uncle Umhlakaza,
and he helped to proclaim the visions. To him and
to others they were, no doubt, expected, and certainly
they were welcome. For what was their message ?
Nongkause had it from the council of spirits, sitting
under the water, a corner of which lifted to allow of
communication.

Disease was making itself felt among the cattle

that formed the main wealth of the Kaffirs. However, the heroic chiefs who had long gone hence, were only waiting to return with endless herds. These were of vastly improved breed, nor could any earthly sickness harm them. From the unknown, there would also arrive all manner of desirable things ; no Kaffir could even imagine them. Finally, those who were to bring the lustrous Kaffraria would march before a giant army. By it, the white would be driven into the sea, and Kaffir rule would direct a Kaffir land.

It was a queen's speech, indeed, that Nongkause put forth ; yet there were conditions attached. Before anything could happen, the Kaffirs must destroy their own cattle, grain, and other belongings, to the utter-most. The chief who had many oxen must slaughter them, and throw the bodies to the wild beasts. The clansman who had a little store of corn must straight-way destroy it. Even the kraals, which gave shelter from the elements, were to be burned down, as if an enemy were being pillaged. Otherwise the new heaven would not appear ; while the starry heaven above, would fall and destroy the disobedient.

'When I heard of the movement,' Sir George Grey narrated, 'I at once hurried north to grapple with it. I could not have believed it so serious, until I was actually on the spot. Kaffraria was in a ferment, and a wave of destruction might roll from it across Cape Colony. Here were nearly a quarter of a million of Kaffirs, a large proportion of whom were busy acting upon the advice of the prophetess. They were destroying their cattle and produce, and looking forward eagerly to a triumph over the whites.

'I went among the chiefs, although warned that I endangered myself unduly, hoping to check the movement. However, it was useless to talk to natives aflame with superstition and passion. Those who doubted the prophetess, would do nothing to keep within bounds, the majority who accepted her as a divinity. Yet, the chiefs invariably received me with kindness, and thanked me for the counsel I gave them. Simply, they could not accept it.'

The Governor adopted every means to place the borders of Cape Colony in a state of military security. As one detail he had to ensure that, in the event of war, the frontier settlers should not be massacred. A line of men was drawn across country, so as to make a buttress against any advance by the crazy Kaffirs. Each picket had charge of a stretch of ground, and in the morning soldiers would ride sharply to right and left, covering it. They could tell, by footmarks on the dewy grass, whether any Kaffirs had been about in the night.

The chief military officer was for falling back upon a less extended position, where he believed he could be more secure. He sought the Governor's authority for the step, which fact well indicates the critical nature of the whole situation. Sir George scribbled an emphatic 'No,' and resumed the scanty sleep from which he had been aroused.

'I had several reasons,' he explained, 'for declining

to permit of any change of our military position. First, it would have been an encouragement to the Kaffirs to attack us, for they would have supposed us in retreat. Second, we should have been leaving open, country where there were European families. Again, the appearance of weakening, on our part, would have driven over the Kaffirs who hesitated, to the side of those who clamoured to attack us. I made it a rule always, and in all things, only to take a step after the most careful and mature thought; but once it had been taken, never to go back upon it. It's a very bad business when you begin to retreat.'

Nothing happened in the manner Nongkause and the wily Umhlakaza had foretold, unless the destruction of Kaffir stock and grain. Two blood-red suns did not flame in the east; neither did the moon, in any of her humours, light the ancient chiefs along, the now precious cattle with them. A mist came up of an afternoon, but no day of darkness followed. Breezes blew, cheering the hot air to freshness; never a hurricane which should break the lintels of the white man's doors. It was weary to wait and starve, with a Governor on the flank, plucking all guidance out of an insurrection.

If the gods of Nongkause had excited a less perfect trust, there might have been a rush on Cape Colony. As it was, the belief lived long enough in the Kaffirs to defeat its own purpose. Their suffering grew acute, nature asserted itself over superstition, and their one cry was 'Give us to eat.' They dug up roots, and they strove for the supplies which the Governor threw into the country, when famine drove Nongkause's nostrum out. Desperate crowds of the hungry surged over hill and plain, while strength lasted, and then lay down to die. No question remained of keeping a mad Kaffraria at bay. The whole effort was to rescue, as far as was possible, the Kaffirs from death by want.

Civilisation drove forward in a mortuary cart ; but it was civilisation. The spirit of Kaffraria had been quenched ; it was a last wild stand. Sir George Grey meditated on the means, so unexpected, so beyond man's control, which had enhanced the securities for peace in South Africa.

He could do that, believing Providence to be an all-wise, if often inscrutable ruler, and at the same time declare : 'There was a heroic element in the action of the Kaffirs, for we see what they were willing to endure at the bidding, as they believed, of their ancestors, and in the interests of themselves as a people.'

It was in Sir George's mind that Nongkause, by a queer irony, was the one member of her family who survived the visitation.

XIV

A SAVIOUR OF INDIA

It touches the imagination to have a dark Africa put forward as light for a Bible scene; namely, that where Jacob, instructed by Rebekah, obtains the blessing which the blind Isaac thinks himself to be conferring on his eldest son Esau.

'This scene,' said Sir George Grey, 'did not live wholly to me, until I met with an incident while hunting in South Africa. Coming upon a young spring-buck, which had been exhausted by the pursuit, I lifted it into the saddle before me, and carried it home. All the way, the velvety skin of the little fellow was brushing against my clothes.

'These were not worn again for some time, and when I did take them out, I was struck by their delicious smell of herbs and grasses. The scent had been communicated by the spring-buck, accustomed to make its home among the sweet growths of nature. It was the hunter's fragrant smell which, in part, caused Isaac to mistake Jacob for Esau.'

While trekking through Cape Colony, to see everybody and everything for himself, Sir George was often able to be the keen sportsman. Before his camp was awake, of a morning, he would make a bowl of black coffee, shoulder his rifle, and start off, with a couple of bush-boys for gillies. He would return in the forenoon, deal with his work as Pro-Consul until the evening, and then, perhaps, seek another shot. Or, if his people were on the move, he might sally from them at one point, and rejoin them later.

Deer of various sorts were not scarce, and he kept the camp larder furnished with fresh meat. The Mahomedans, among his motley following, ate with relish the product of his rifle.

'They trusted me,' he dwelt on that, ' to say " In the name of the Lord," when a beast was killed, so observing the Mahomedan rite. They would not have eaten of its flesh, had they not known that their belief was expressed, " You are not to destroy one of the Creator's creatures, except by His permission." Whenever Mahomedans were with me, I undertook to observe the rule, nor did I ever fail.'

One sees, in that fact of chance mention, another evidence of how Sir George came to be such a force among the raw men of the earth. He had the genius for taking pains to understand them, and thus, even unwittingly, made them his disciples. Just, he touched the spot.

In his reign at the Cape, the lion was still rampant far south of the Zambesi. Twice, while hunting, he got on the trail of the monarch, but he never slew him. A leopard would skulk into the demesne of

Table Mountain itself, and be ingloriously trapped.
The lion made other sport, lying on a high place
while it was day, and going forth to roam at dark.
Sir George went to the Bible for the character sketch
of the lion, in particular to the Psalms :

> Thou makest darkness, and it is night ;
> Wherein all the beasts of the forest do creep forth.
> The young lions roar after their prey,
> And seek their meat from God :
> The sun ariseth, they gather themselves together,
> And lay them down in their dens.

There was a hill, with a wide outlook of plain,
and from it, the lesser wild animals at feed, might be
marked for the gloaming. It was covert wherein the
lion could abide, to lie in wait, a secret lurking-place.
Up the back of this hill climbed Sir George, eye and
ear on the alert, for one suspected to be about. He
was about, but already bounding down the rocky face
of the ridge, in a hurry to be clear of the hunter.
Sir George mounted his horse, eager to cut him off,
and rode, break-neck, the path he had already climbed.
There the lion galloped, at a kingly swing, heading for
the thick bush in the distance. As he neared it, Sir
George aimed a forlorn shot, which proved a farewell
salute. He dismounted, and waded through the
growth, to the concern of his Kaffir boy, but the lion
was tracked no more.

These excursions of a leisure hour sent Sir George
fresh, vigorous, full of resource to the alarums that
arraigned him in South Africa. The greatest of them

was not South African, but blew across the Indian Ocean. On an August morning, a steamer drew wearily into Table Bay with a message for the Governor. It was an express from Lord Elphinstone at Bombay, red-bordered, in that it told of the tremendous affair now calmly fixed in history as the Indian Mutiny. Here was an earnest cry, 'Come over and help us,' addressed to the potent British satrap nearest in the Seven Seas.

'Yes,' Sir George mentioned, 'the dispatch was in no wise positive as to the outlook in India. Trouble there had been and would be; that was certain. But was India merely face to face with a disturbance which she could manage herself, or was it a widespread mutiny? I was really left to form my own view upon the situation, and I decided that things were very serious. Apparently, religious motives were at the bottom of the affair, and I could fancy how fanaticism, bred thereon, might sweep India. My responsibilities in South Africa were great, for the mad Kaffir movement had hardly been stayed; nay, my whole surroundings were as a thicket of thorns, in their possible complications. But India, which might be lost to us, outweighed everything else, and I felt it my duty to contribute assistance to the utmost limit of my resources.' ·

He would ship troops, guns, munitions, specie, everything South Africa could give, off to India. While he was doing it, a more splendid thing happened—his masterful laying hands upon the troopships passing the Cape for China, and his sending of them to India instead. 'I have,' he recorded the act at the time, 'directed that all vessels arriving here with troops for China, shall proceed direct to Calcutta instead of to Singapore.' They are laconic words, but their place is over the front door of the British Empire. To it they brought a service, not ordinary in its annals, as they marked a man willing to put all to the touch. A nation and a personality are in the incident, and, remembering that, let us trace it out.

At this date we had a variance with China, and were undertaking warlike operations in that country, jointly with France. Troops from England were hurrying to Lord Elgin, who was seeing our affairs through in China. Some of the transports reached Cape Town, a few days after Sir George Grey received the Elphinstone message. They needed water and fresh provisions, and receiving these would have gone on with all haste to China. It was a throbbing moment for a Cape Governor, accustomed to think in the British Empire. What should he do ?

You can fancy him working out his course, like a master mariner taking the stars. Nor, must the process occupy longer. He was rapidly dispatching the forces which were at his command in South Africa. This might prove rash, having regard to the state of the country. Events might confuse him, and be his downfall. Still, he was not going beyond the bounds of his commission, and there were the specious reasons why South Africa should fly to the aid of India.

He set them out then, and their reperusal, in the armchair of his London retirement, but emphasised their purport. As a great empire, set hither and thither, could only be governed by the free consent of all concerned, so it must be a unit when danger threatened any part. Here was the British Empire, a vast area, scattered over the globe. It was essential that everybody should see it had not overgrown its strength. Be manifest that its vitality, its power of action, were as keen at the extremities as at the centre. Should a portion be gravely endangered, the world must behold all the other sections stirring themselves to meet the emergency. Each should be a leader for the whole body, the supreme weight of which would thus be focussed upon the menaced quarter. In the process, our varied peoples would determine their common interests and a common pride of dominion, incalculable in worth.

Within this singleness of the Empire, came Colonel Adrian Hope and his gallant 93rd Highlanders, then at Cape Town on their way to China. Only, Sir George Grey's commission, as Cape Governor, gave him no authority to divert, from its mission, an oversea military expedition. He would be stepping outside his own realm with a vengeance, because he would be superseding the orders of the British Government. The contemplation of such a step was staggering. But would it be wisdom ? That decided, it should go through, for Sir George did not bind himself by forms or consequences. Never being an official, than which no truer word could be writ, he was wont to give ready hostage to his official fortunes. India was to top all.

The meagre information from there, left him, as has been seen, to act very much on possibilities. These, however, were dark and storm-laden ; he felt that England was confronted by her whole destiny in India. On the other hand, the operations in China were the result of a compact with France. To deflect troops elsewhere, might be a serious breach of that compact. It was so easy not to do anything ; Sir George resolved to do everything.

'I informed Adrian Hope,' he described the result, 'of the apparent state of affairs in India, and of the course which seemed to me necessary. This was that he must proceed direct from Cape Town to Calcutta, instead of following his existing orders. Should there be no need for him at Calcutta, he could continue his voyage to Singapore, with a loss of time not material. Quite naturally, he was doubtful as to what he ought to do. He was under orders for a theatre of war, and was responsible to his superiors in London.

'I undertook the full authority for the change which I urged, and I remarked that unless he accepted my direction, it would most likely be refused by other officers arriving at Cape Town. He agreed to do as I wished, on condition that I put my commands in writing, and this I did at once. The noble fellow arrived in India in the nick of time, as did the forces which had previously left South Africa. Sir Colin Campbell was enabled, being so strengthened, to complete his expedition for the relief of Lucknow.

'I caused a steamer to cruise out from Cape Town, to intercept other troopships and send them on to China. While I was thus steadily forwarding relief to India, I learned that Canning, the Governor-General, was still hopeful of avoiding grave trouble. At that I was anxious lest, after all, I had misjudged the situation and the demands upon myself to meet it. Next, I had full tidings from India, and I knew that my efforts, twice over, would have been useful. India was in the balance.'

Sir George had to keep the peace in turbulent Kaffraria with a mere remnant of soldiers. The colonists, anxious to assist the relief of India, took sentry-go at Cape Town in place of the regulars. It was all a knitting of the Empire; the uniting of its strands by blood and bone and sentiment; that federation, based on race and the human qualities, which had budded and bloomed in Sir George Grey's mind.

'For instance,' he wrote from Cape Town, 'there is not one of the gentlemen in this part of the country who will now, in his turn, abandon his bed, to sleep for the night in the guardhouse, and to walk his beat as sentry, who will not think that he has made some sacrifice for Her Majesty's honour and for the safety of even a distant part of the Empire, and who will not henceforth regard any persons that assail the interests of the Queen, or her possessions, very much in the light of personal antagonists. In fact, all here now feel that they are useful members of a great body corporate, in which they have their personal interest, which arises from having made some sacrifices to promote the common good of the whole. Such a feeling, pervading the Empire, must immeasurably increase its strength, unity, and stability.'

Sir George sent his own carriage horses to India, there to be yoked to smoking guns, and went afoot in Cape Town. The maintenance of peace, among the pugnacious chiefs of South Africa, depended mainly upon his personal influence with them. He borrowed horses and rode round among those chiefs, binding them over, in their only recognisances, as honourable men, not to disturb the country. It was a strange Pax Britannica ; an affair of novel, almost quixotic, elements. But it went through royally.

'You know,' one fancies Sir George delivering himself during his circuit of the kraals, 'the Queen, for whom I speak, has to quell a rising which threatens all that is good in one of her other possessions. Those who fight against her are of exceeding number, while her forces there are comparatively few. Now, you are all warriors of experience who, if there must be fighting, would like to see a fair contest. In England the Queen has many soldiers, but England is as far again from India as we are. Thus, I can send troops from here in less time, and I am doing so, relying upon you, as gentlemen, to see that the peace is kept while they are away. With you, therefore, I leave that trust, mindful that we are all subjects of a Queen who loves those who serve her loyally, but who, when justly angered, can strike heavily.'

The velvet glove, fastening with the steel button, was gladly taken up by the chiefs, nor did they betray the Governor's confidence. His invasion of Moshesh, in this relation, was quite an exploit, for the old fellow was stern and wily. Sir George had brought about the cease fire, in a quarrel between the Basutos and the Boers. That gave him the prestige which was requisite for anyone who would go to Thaba Bosigo. Having a Boer for guide, and a few natives for retinue, the Governor presented himself at the outer postern of the stronghold, after darkness had fallen.

' I was admitted,' he said, 'and found Moshesh ill in bed, a bright nightcap, with a tassel, on his head. A more strange, more picturesque conference, bearing upon the well-being of the British Empire, surely never took place. Moshesh was propped up in his bed, his leading men grouped themselves round, and we talked. A fire burned in the place, a tallow candle or two spluttered, making lights and shadows as in a Rembrandt picture. My natives understood Basuto and English, and were the medium for my converse with Moshesh. He was really one of the cleverest fellows in all South Africa, as well as one of the most powerful

chiefs. Thus, I was pleased with myself when I left
Thaba Bosigo, no longer a Mountain of Midnight,
knowing that he was in my league of peace.'

This novel covenant was strictly observed by the
chiefs, so assuring the Governor against his next venture. It hurled him, once more, through the fabric
of the British constitution, a road to which he had
grown familiar. What should he do but raise two
regiments on his own mandate, a usurpation of the
sovereign rights. It occurred in this fashion.

Bombay had not taken the distemper, rife in such
a large area of India. However, Lord Elphinstone
learned that a Bombay rising had been arranged for a
certain religious festival. He had not forces enough left
him to overawe the populace, or, failing that, to cope
with an outbreak. He despatched another express to
Sir George Grey, at the Cape, to the effect : ' I know
you have already denuded South Africa of troops, but
I am hoping you may somehow manage to help us
against this Bombay crisis.'

Sir George bethought himself of the men, formerly
composing the German Legion, who were settled
in the Colony. He collected these with what other
recruits he could entice, formed them into regiments,
and sent them to Bombay. ' I signed the commissions
for the officers,' he recalled, ' but I'm afraid my signature would have meant nothing, after the ships were
on the high sea. In the event of the men creating a
disturbance, the officers would really have had no legal
authority to quell it.' He communicated with the

East India Company, desiring that the regiments should be put on a regular footing immediately they reached Bombay.

'For raising the regiments,' Sir George continued, 'I was charged at home with a breach of the constitution. It was all that. I got word that I should learn by a later mail what was to be the upshot. A friendly member of the Government wrote me a note beginning : "Dear Grey, you have done for yourself at last ; I always feared it would come to this." My own position was very plain. Here was an unconstitutional thing, but a necessary thing.

'Meanwhile I had news from Bombay, that it was the provident arrival of the Germans which, most likely, prevented the outbreak that had been feared. I put the dispatch in my pocket, with the reflection : "Ah, they can now interfere with me from London if they will ! " There, I judged, they had similar information from Bombay, for I heard nothing farther as to what was to be done with me.

'When the first tidings of the trouble in India reached me, I laid it down that all previous orders and directions from England were cancelled. These had been given before the new position arose, and were, in my judgment, overborne by the new perils.

'As for myself, in a personal way, I felt that I should not feel it a disgrace to be recalled for doing what I regarded as my duty. I had not very much, but, at the worst, I had enough to live upon.'

Without a masterful Pro-Consul at the Cape,

Lucknow might have fallen, before there were forces to relieve it. That would have lit, for our rule in India, a bonfire in which Bombay would only have been a crackling twig.

It was a stirring British tune that the kilted pipers of the 93rd at Lucknow played.

XV

AYE DREAMING AND DOING

CARLYLE and Sir George Grey, forgathered at
Chelsea, walked up and down in the open, as they
often did, discussing some religious question. Carlyle
stopped, laid his hand on Sir George's shoulder, and,
looking him in the face, exclaimed, ' Oh, that I could
believe like you ! '

Well, no plank in the faith of Sir George was
more firm than the one marked : ' Mission and destiny
of the Anglo-Saxon people.' He had been planting
the outposts of empire, and he saw these grow out
towards each other. Then, he beheld the old Mother-
land and them, twining ever closer into a mighty
garland, which should sweeten the globe with
fragrance. Nay, he even saw again, in the garland,
a very radiant bloom that a king's tempest had
sundered.

' In effect,' said Sir George, ' I was recalled from
South Africa, on account of proposals I had made,
towards federation in that part of the realm. I
planned to federate, for common action, Cape Colony,
Natal, our other territories, and also the Orange Free

State. Farther, I had virtually asked the co-operation of the Transvaal Republic, with the Government and people of which, I was on very friendly terms. There was to be no change anywhere; simply, a federal Parliament would manage affairs that were of concern to all parties. I have little doubt that I could have brought about federation, only I was not permitted to go on. Much as my proposals were supported in South Africa, I could get no hearing for them from my superiors at home.'

It had been the same when, in New Zealand, he took steps to paint all the Pacific Isles, British. He wanted the Pacific, then largely an unstaked claim, to have our flag flying in solitary peace. Thus the smaller sections of the New World, like the larger areas, should be led onward, undisturbed by the rivalries of the Old World. Fill the lap of England with distant lands, but exact from her the most sublime service to them—that of a mother. If Sir George had been supported, New Caledonia would have entered the British nursery.

'I had,' that lost part of our history ran, 'regarded the New Caledonian group as pertaining to New Zealand. Making a tour of the Pacific Islands, with Bishop Selwyn, I visited New Caledonia. We had no representative there, and three days before our arrival, a French frigate had put in and hoisted the French flag.

'I protested against that, in an official letter to the French captain. He declared his orders from the

French Government to be specific ; he was to annex New Caledonia. I had an old brig, while he had a good man-of-war. No doubt I could have spoken with more authority, if my vessel had also been a man-of-war. However, as a result of my representations, it was arranged that the French should do nothing, incur no expenditure, which would interfere with the island being declared British, until we had referred the matter to our Governments.

'This was about the time of the agreement, between ourselves and Louis Napoleon, in reference to the invasion of the Crimea. It is conceivable, that the French Emperor took advantage of the opportunity to lay hands on New Caledonia. Anyhow, I feared that the alliance might counteract my despatch to London. Most likely it did, for I was instructed that the French were to be left in possession.'

While sailing the Pacific, Sir George also called at Norfolk Island, then a prison house. The worst characters of the Australian penal settlements, those to whom perdition beaconed, were drafted to Norfolk Island. The whole scene shocked Sir George, as it rankled in his memory, a sombre nightmare. It saddened him, to think that so fair a place should be one of the black spots of the earth.

'Here,' he said, 'were nature and man meeting together, she at her best, he at his worst. How beautiful we found Norfolk Island ; how well graced, with its pine and other trees ! I suppose there is no tree, growing anywhere, which for beauty could be given preference over the Norfolk Island pine. It was an evidence of the bounteous garden, set by nature amid a fresh, crystal sea, and wooed by a loving climate.

'By contrast, the convict settlement! The stricken creatures worked in irons, and when evening came, they were turned into a great court where they slept. The irons being, in most instances, removed, the quarrelling and fighting began. I heard of a convict who had been tried for killing a fellow, during some fall-out. He appealed to those judging him : "I came here, having the heart of a man, and your convict system, with its brutal associations, has given me the heart of a beast."'

England built in tribulations—nations! At first we had no better use for Australia than to moor hulks to it. That was an eddy in the nobler stream of tribulation which, like the Nile, bore all fertility in its waters. Sir George Grey sat upon a Mount Pisgah that commanded the past and the future. He saw the stream, beginning in far-away mist-crowned sources, roll down the ages. It was a flood of destiny.

'I suppose,' he submitted, 'we all recognise that there are certain driving forces behind the march of humanity. We may not see them, or we may merely get a glimpse of them now and then, but they are there, and always in operation. Providence ; that is my word. The chief of these forces we have, as I hold, in the evolution of the Anglo-Saxon race.'

Go back to the England of Elizabeth, and what

did we find? A race of hardy men, who took delight in sailing virgin seas, in becoming familiar with new countries; who were opening up fresh tracks across the globe. Following upon that, consider the drift of legislation in the British Isles, from the period of Elizabeth. It was to appropriate the land into the hands of a few, to create great landlords, to make individual men the owners, nay the tyrants, of vast areas. This meant depriving the common people of their natural means of subsistence. It forced them to maintain themselves where there was actually no room, with the outcrop of want, suffering, discontent.

The great eating up of the Irish land, the throttling of the natural wealth of that country, began with the ill work done in the Elizabethan age. Yet, the full mischief did not appear until Sir George's own early days, when the Irish people were leaving their native land in shiploads. In England the result came sooner, and ran on continuously, rather than burst the wave which was to engulf Ireland.

'Has it ever occurred to you,' Sir George asked, 'how beautiful a contribution the Irish girl, driven to another land by starvation, has made to the development of the English-speaking race? What a stretch of Anglo-Saxondom has been peopled by her wages, hardly earned in service, and sent home to Ireland for the emigration of her father and mother, her sisters and brothers! She is a winning illustration of how the hard task-master necessity, has been our architect for building up new nations. Ireland has been tortured and beaten, and her daughters and sons, in that torture, those blows, have done wondrous work for us.

Coupled with divorce between the people and the land, there arose in the British Isles, religious persecutions and tyrannies. These were the twin forces which, with just exception enough to prove the rule, planted the Anglo-Saxon in every corner of the earth. Two great evils working out in good; a sowing in wrong and wickedness, the garnering righteousness.

Cradling like that made men and nations. When Spain founded colonies, she sent delegates designedly to do so. When France colonised Canada, that was her model; and the like with other nations. They planted all the Old World institutions, with their imperfections, on new soil, which, as time had shown, was like building on sand.

Taught by bitter experience at home, Anglo-Saxons struck out fresh lines, in the fresh lands where, thanks to the discoveries of adventurous rovers, they could find asylum. The humanities in them got scope; they carried tolerance and liberty ever with them. Take the Puritans who founded New England! Was there ever such a noble band? Again, take the Quakers or the English and Irish Roman Catholics! In some cases, when there was persecution on the Continent of Europe, these British emigrants attracted to them what was perse-

cuted. South Africa was founded in oppression, in-
dependently of us as it happened, since the forefathers
of the Boers were largely French Huguenots.

It was not enough, that the Anglo-Saxon should
rush from starvation and persecution, to a freer home
across the seas. No sooner had he found it, than
the old oppression might again be clanking its chains
at his heels. The stern Mother more than once
stretched out her hand to coerce her freer children,
forcing them ever to take new ground, and be, so
to speak, clear of her clutches. The instance of
America, occurred during this second stage in the weft
and woof of tribulation which was at the root of
our growth. The same with the Boers of South
Africa, who, by harsh regulations, were forced inland,
thus opening up new territory. It had all worked
with the precision and force of a Nasmyth hammer.

Naturally, a time would arrive when the liberty
and freedom of the Saxon, gone over sea, should
react upon the Old World. Sir George held it
proven that the inspiration of the New World had,
in real measure, been the emancipation of the Old.
Very many of the inventions of the nineteenth
century, which were the threads of modern progress,
were to have their origin in the New World. She
would heap coals of fire on the head of the Old.

How to help this girdling of the whole world
with beneficent influences, through the medium of
the Anglo-Saxon ? Sir George turned him on his
Mount Pisgah, first in New Zealand, later in South

Africa. He had been looking at the scored, furrowed, violent past. It had worked out its meaning, nor was there doubt as to the bearing of that message upon the future.

At Pisgah's highest peak the sun shone, only there were mists, which it did not pierce, in the valleys below. Just, it caught one wisp of the vapour, and twirled it about in the wind. The errant thing flung into a sign—Federation of the English-speaking People ; and was gone.

Sir George Grey dipped for a Grand Pacific Isles Protectorate, and a red noose from Downing Street strangled it. He dipped for a Federated South Africa, and the red noose caught himself. That is, he was recalled from his Cape Governorship on account of his projects. Ah, that he had been permitted to go on with them ! All the gold of the Randt would not have weighed in the scales like that.

True, he was returned to South Africa, which clamoured angrily at his recall, but, as he said, 'It was with strict injunctions to stop my federation schemes, for these would not be tolerated.'

They were a generation too soon. Yet, their author had already drawn on posterity in order to develop English colonies. Was it right to tax posterity ? High talk turned on this at a dinner in London, where Sir George met Gladstone, Macaulay, and other celebrities. 'Certainly,' Sir George argued, ' if some large expense is undertaken which will benefit those to come after us, as well as those already here, it

is mere equity that the former should be charged with
their share.' The principle had been put into practice
in the Colonies, and he imagined that this dinner
helped its advance in the Old Country. Especially, he
applied that opinion to the taking over, by Government,
of the English telegraph lines.

'I recall very well,' Sir George stated, 'the
picturesque way in which Macaulay expressed our
common trait of being interested in trifles that affect
us closely, to the neglect of large happenings which
are distant. " Here," he said, about some item of news,
" is a mandarin in China who has beheaded a thousand
people in a batch. I was quite shocked when I read of
it this morning. During the day I contrived to cut one
of my fingers. I'm ashamed to confess that I thought so
much about the finger, that I quite forgot the massacred
Chinamen !" That was Macaulay's illustration.

' As the dinner party was breaking up, I stood for
a minute with him. He had not been enjoying very
good health. When I congratulated him on his
seeming revival in strength, he showed me his hand,
which was puffy and blown, and answered : " Oh, I'm
not so well as you might think." Poor fellow, the
remark was too true, for he died within a fortnight
from that evening.'

To South Africa, soon after Sir George Grey had
resumed duty there, came a member of the royal
family. This was Prince Alfred, later the Duke of
Edinburgh, now the Duke of Saxe-Coburg-Gotha.
Sir George suggested the visit, and he believed it had

excellent results. It delighted the colonists to have a son of the Queen among them. Seeing him the natives could exclaim, 'Again, the Queen loves us or she would not send us her son!' The visit drew out the regard of South Africa towards England and its Sovereign. Certainly the federal idea!

'Prince Alfred,' Sir George made an appreciation of him, 'was a nice, frank, handsome boy; an excessively taking little boy. In his honour, we had perhaps the largest hunt that ever took place in South Africa. It was calculated that he shot more deer in fifteen minutes, than his father would have shot in the Scottish Highlands in a season.

'The Prince had to face a different sort of experience at a town, Port Elizabeth I think, which we reached on his birthday. He had to walk between lines of girls, laden with bouquets, which they flung down before him, to the words : "Many happy returns of the day." It was rather trying for a midshipman.

'Everybody was delighted with Prince Alfred, and even the President of the Transvaal Republic called him "Our Prince." For his progress through the country, I had a beautiful wagon made. At the close of the tour Prince Alfred gave it, a friendly gift, to the Transvaal President. You can understand how it would be regarded by him, even be useful. Moreover it was calculated, while only a wagon, to impress the burghers of the Transvaal with the greatness of England. A simple pastoral people, they could not themselves have begot such a vehicle and team.'

PRINCE ALFRED

Prince Alfred confided to Sir George Grey, with boyish certainty, that he never wanted to succeed to the Duchy of Saxe-Coburg. He wouldn't have it.

'I have been all over the place,' exclaimed the dashing young sailor, 'and, believe me, it hasn't a pond on which you could sail a punt.'

XVI

THE FAR-FLUNG BATTLE-LINE

A CAPTAIN of the sea most proves himself that when it storms, and so a captain of empire.

The danger signal was flying again in New Zealand, and Sir George Grey must needs be asked to get it down. Hardly had he been keel-hauled for his doings in one colony, when another required him. He must have been uncertain whether to despair or smile. It was like love-making.

During his first rule in New Zealand, Sir George held a conference of Maori chiefs, Te Whero Whero being present. He had come along, in the train of the Governor, without any of his own people, who lived farther north. It grieved him to be thus situate, at a crisis when the ability to tender assistance in men, might be of the utmost worth.

'Those other chiefs,' he addressed Sir George, 'are all inferior to me, but they have their retainers with them. They are promising you to bring so much strength into the field, while, for myself, I have no one here. I seem not to aid you at all, but as long as I am separated from my own people I'll fight in the ranks of some other chief. You have treated me badly, in that I am here without support to give you. You force me to put myself in quite a humble position.'

The speech was esteemed by Sir George at more than warriors, and the memory of it made him exclaim : ' Ah, they were fine fellows, those old Maori chieftains ! You required to understand them, but they were worth every study ; nobles of a noble race ! '

Meanwhile, Te Whero Whero had died. A concert of tribes had made him Maori King, and his son Tawhiao succeeded to the newly set up throne. It was the symbol of a movement to keep the Maori nation intact, though land rights were the immediate subject of clash. Many things had happened while Sir George Grey was in South Africa ; he was the problem-solver called in late.

' You might put it broadly,' he expressed the problem, ' that the Maoris were making a last stand for their fatherland, and credit be to them in that sense. They, no doubt, wished to be full governors of New Zealand, and they talked of driving out the Europeans. I set to work, with my best energies, to smooth away the troubles which threatened so thickly.'

Sir George went quietly among the disaffected natives, hence a dramatic scene at the graveside of Te Whero Whero. He journeyed alone to the Maori headquarters, feeling that he was in no danger. When he arrived, the place was almost deserted, the Maoris being elsewhere in council. He sought out the grave of Te Whero Whero, bowed his head in tribute over it, and there stood to ruminate on old associations. Thus the Maoris discovered him, to their astonishment, and they cried : 'Come here ! Come here ! ' If there had been no welcome for him the Maori cry would have been : 'Go away ! Go away ! '

'Word of my presence,' Sir George remembered, 'was sent to King Tawhiao, and he started to ride to me, but was unable, being worn out, to complete his journey. With royal etiquette, he had a certificate to that purport made out and sent on to me for my satisfaction. It was drawn up and attested with every precision, and I got it all right, nor could I help laughing at the idea.

'But Tawhiao's anxiety that I should be assured of his good faith, even in so trifling a matter, struck me as a pleasing item of character. I took a fancy to him after we became personally acquainted, and he was one of the last persons I saw, when I finally left New Zealand for England. Years before, I had bidden him another good-bye, he being then the one who was setting out on a visit to England.'

Estimated by his name, Tawhiao was a 'scorner of the sun,' but unhappily not of spirits. They were apt, in the days when his kingship had grown an empty name, to make him quite unkingly. He naturally called upon Sir George Grey, for years out of official life, to learn about England.

'Will you answer me a question ?' Sir George

broached him, adding : 'There need be no false modesty between friends.'

Tawhiao waited sedately for the question, which was : 'What would you think of a man who, by some wrong means, had brought about the death of a fellow-being ? '

'Why, he would be a very bad man ; a man deserving of most severe punishment.'

'If a man brought about the death of several other men, what would you say ? '

'Who could be so cruel ? It is not possible that anybody could be so wicked.'

'If that is your view, Tawhiao, what words would you have for a man who destroyed the happiness of a whole nation, and that his own ? '

Tawhiao could not frame words for such a person, more especially as he now began to realise that the parables were fitting himself. 'Yes, yes,' was his exclamation, 'I understand, I understand ! ' Then he cried like a baby.

What judgment would England pass upon King Tawhiao if, while a visitor there, he gave way to drink ? He would disgrace, not himself only, but the whole Maori race.

'Alas, yes,' sobbed Tawhiao; 'what can be done ? '

'I'll tell you,' said Sir George gently. 'We'll both sign a pledge, agreeing to abstain from alcohol in any form. That pledge will mutually bind us for a term of years, and there could be no more sacred contract.'

It was a bright contract for Tawhiao. And now here he was, at a New Zealand wayside station, where there drew up the train carrying Sir George Grey, on his last New Zealand journey, to the Plymouth-bound liner. 'I wished him farewell,' Sir George described this parting, 'and he wept. I was much touched, remembering that he had been all through a Maori war against me.'

That was retrospect. The second Maori war afforded Sir John Gorst an experience not without humour.

In Sir George Grey's phrase, Sir John Gorst went out to New Zealand to do good and did it. He conducted a school for the education of the Maoris, and acted as Government Commissioner. 'He had been at work for some time,' Sir George added, 'and had achieved excellent results altogether. He was popular with the Maoris, and indeed they never had a truer friend.' However, some of those ardent in the 'king movement,' regarded his mere presence in the heart of their territory, as an influence against its success. The crisis arrived from an encounter of wits which fairly set the Waikato river on fire.

'The Maoris,' Sir George retailed this affair, 'had founded a paper to propagate the king movement. They christened it by a name which might be freely translated as " The Giant Eagle Flying Aloft." With my approval, Sir John Gorst brought out a protagonist to the Maori weekly. I furnished the requisites for the venture, the money coming from revenues applicable to native purposes.

'The idea was to counteract the teaching of the
"Giant Eagle Flying Aloft"; to show how absurd it
was for any section of the Maoris to think they
could beat the English. Our organ was designed to
be educative, and in that respect to help in the maintenance of peace. The title of the Maori paper was
in allusion to a great eagle, which, at a remote period,
had existed in New Zealand. The Maoris had
chants about it, and in their legends it was described
as "Bed-fellow of earth-shaking thunder."

'Very well, Sir John Gorst replied to their grand
title by another in Maori, signifying : "The Lonely
Sparrow on the House Top." This, of course, was
suggested by the Scriptures, and its force of contrast
at once tickled the Maori sense of humour. Sir
John Gorst's satire was so keen that they could not,
themselves, help laughing over the fun which "The
Lonely Sparrow on the House Top" made of "The
Giant Eagle Flying Aloft." It went on for several
numbers, perhaps half-a-dozen, when the Maoris
informed Sir John that he must stop his paper, or they
would throw his printing materials into the river.

'The conductors of "The Giant Eagle Flying
Aloft" had the view, if I am not mistaken, that
"The Lonely Sparrow on the House Top" did not
fight with adequate dignity. It was too anxious to
make merriment of its adversary, so causing the
latter to appear ridiculous to many Maoris. Sir John

Gorst paid no heed to the threats against him, and next, there arrived a band of Maoris who uprooted his printing machinery. He happened to be from home at the time, and when he returned it was to find this disorder, and the Maoris in possession.

'The scheme thus to dispossess him and the "Lonely Sparrow on the House Top," had been headed by the chief Rewi. It was Rewi who flung, from a besieged pa, the defiant message that the Maoris would never surrender, that they would fight "For ever, For ever, For ever!" I am inclined to believe that he put himself at the head of the raid upon Sir John Gorst, in order to be able to protect him from any hurt.'

Be that as it might, Rewi and the raiders were determined that Sir John Gorst should depart the 'king country.' They pronounced this verdict upon him with every ceremony, and his answer was equally determined. It was : 'Nothing but a direct order from Sir George Grey shall induce me to leave my post.' At that, Rewi granted time for a reference to the Governor, who instructed Sir John Gorst to withdraw. Had it been otherwise, or had the order lagged, Sir John would most likely have shared the fate of 'The Lonely Sparrow on the House Top !' The sword proved mightier than the pen in that duel.

And despite Sir George Grey's efforts, the sword was again to be drawn over a wide area of New Zealand. A particular land dispute, which meant cleavage with the confederated Maoris, had been gnawing its way along. Sir George investigated it, reached the decision that the Maori claim was just, and made up his mind to rescind the purchase. He was not autocrat now, as he had been before, the New Zealand constitution which he had drafted, being in operation. Things had to move by routine, there was muddling somewhere, and in the middle of it all, the Maoris waylaid a small party of soldiers.

Nobody had dreamt of such a thing. Sir George's ministers asked him : 'What are you going to do after this outrage and challenge ? ' He answered : ' We must give the land back, according to promise. The duty of a powerful State is to be just, and reintroduce the proper owner to the land. We cannot refuse to do so, because persons, over whom he has no control, have massacred our soldiers.' But war surged across New Zealand, a wild, unwholesome spectre, and Sir George must take it so. It had the tale of Wereroa Pa, which again presents him as the mailed hand.

A British officer held a post which could not be relieved, until the Maoris in Wereroa Pa had been scattered. That enforced the necessity, urgent enough in itself, for capturing the fortress. The Maoris had spent all their craft of defence on Wereroa, as, in the former New Zealand war, they did on Ruapekapeka. Engirt by palisades of wood, high and strong, they cried defiance to the Pakeha. The general in control of the British troops would not tackle Wereroa with the strength at his disposal. Sir George Grey resolved to do it himself, and got together what force he could. It was bestriding the military regulations, usurping all forms and traditions, but it was war.

The Maoris in the pa had a passing mind to surrender, and Sir George was anxious to catch them thus. He rode up to take possession, though those with him counselled, 'Be careful lest we come to grief.' The parley was perilous, for the bulk of the Maoris inside the pa were inclined, after all, to resist to the uttermost. Sir George and his escort drew up within easy range of the Maori muskets, and he was loth to turn back. He only did so, when it had become evident that further delay might bring a disaster.

'I wanted to convince them,' he emphasised, 'that if they would not give up the place we should have to take it. Our welcome was so risky that we might, perhaps, be compared to the little boy who scrambled up a garden wall, only to find himself face to face with the Scotch gardener. "Where are you going?" demanded the gardener; and the boy answered, "Back again."

'That was our situation; we must return, since nothing could be achieved by debate. No, I don't think that I had any bodily feeling as to the danger we ran, any burden of danger. Nobody can be afraid who has the lives of others hanging upon his actions. A man who every instant is applied to for orders, has not time to think of fear. It finds scope when a person is acting under the direction of somebody else, and thus is ignorant of the measures being carried out for the common protection and success. Ignorance is ever the channel through which fear attacks a human being, as watch a little child when it understands, and when it does not.'

Perhaps Sir George Grey's nearest passage with death, in Maoriland, occurred during the first war, but he did not learn of it until later. 'I was,' he said, 'in the habit every forenoon of riding between our military camp and the sea-shore, where the war-ships lay at anchor. Having regard to the unsettled state of the country, it was maybe imprudent of me to do this, and moreover I was only accompanied by an orderly sergeant. It seemed that some Maoris hid in wait for me in a valley, intending, I am afraid, to fire upon me. Two things fortunately happened. I rode down very early that day, and some turn of duty took me back by another road. Then, it proved to be the last day on which it was necessary for me to communicate with the ships. Good luck attended me, as I congratulated myself, when informed of the plot and its failure by a Maori who had knowledge of it. Upon what slight chances do things depend ! No, they only seem so to depend !'

As to Wereroa, it must be captured by strength of arms, or rather by a subtle use of these. There could be no idea of attacking it from the front. That would have been a funeral march for Sir George's handful of men. He devised the capture of a rough

spur of ground which commanded the pa. The
Maoris built square to a hostile world, and forgot this
height behind them. If it should be attained, they
were out-manœuvred and helpless. The British fighting men, with Maori allies, marched off to break in
upon the rear of the Wereroa. They filed past the
Governor, shaking hands with him ; the moment was
tense.

'Assuredly,' Sir George remarked, 'the mission
was not without danger, as what venture can be in
war ? Only, my people must have felt that I would
not put them to it, unless there was every hope of
success. That little parade brought up thoughts in
all of us, and was very touching.'

The vital spur was captured, and with it a cohort
of Maoris who were marching to relieve the pa.
The garrison of Wereroa were beaten by tactics, the
most deadly of weapons, and they accepted the verdict.
The victory was the more complete, in that the
Governor lost never a man of his tiny army. It
would be hard to aver that he did not, even as the
grave Pro-Consul, love such an adventure for itself.
That tune sang in the blood.

Here a signpost is reached. Thirty years had
passed, since Sir George Grey waded into the surf
where savagery and civilisation meet, stilling it for the
latter. The harness of empire on him, had been at
full strain all the time. He had come through the
passes, alike in the conduct of wars, and in the higher
mission of spreading light and happiness on the wings

of peace. But much sunshine had covered his track, and it was a light which would not fail.

> What think'st thou of our Empire now, though earn'd
> With travail difficult ?

No, the cold hand of Downing Street intervened ; his second Governorship of New Zealand slammed to a close. It was an era when the Imperial spirit was niggardly, obscurantist. Brushing aside details, it is easy to see how the servant and the official masters, choosing different roads, would ultimately part.

The 'dangerous man' was outcast, and thereon he said in ripeness : 'If my going was equivalent to recall, I have nothing to regret in what I did. Farther, I think history has vindicated my work as a whole.'

XVII

FOR ENGLAND'S SAKE

'Suppose,' urged Sir George Grey, 'that in my life-time a hundred men have died from disappointment and chagrin—that is enough to condemn the whole system!'

He was speaking of Disraeli's discovery, that the great colonial Governorships should go to those who had been 'born in the purple' or had married into it. It was, in a way, a matter personal to him, because the plan came into operation about the date his Pro-Consulship ceased. He felt that possibly it influenced the manner of his going, and, if so, that a wrong was done him as an individual. But he was merely bringing out his attitude to the system itself.

'I thought it was bad for everybody. In effect, it shut the field against simple merit; anyhow, discouraged it. A person might have all the qualities for a Governorship, except part and parcel in the peerage. On the other hand, it was injurious to the Colonies, because it set up men on an eminence, not for sheer merit, but because they happened to be born to rank. How did Napoleon Bonaparte make his army?

By opening the very highest places to whoever could best fill them.'

Governor or no Governor, Sir George Grey must still work for his ideas and ideals, and after a little he hied him to England. Thinking, perhaps, that it had been abrupt with him, Downing Street was affable and kindly. But he was never, no matter how British Governments came or went, to be more employed. South Africa yearned for a strong pilot, and he was ready to step aboard. 'I even asked,' he said, 'to be sent back there, the one occasion on which I ever asked for anything, but without result.'

Disraeli offered to find him a seat in Parliament, perhaps as a sort of balm for wounded feelings. 'I put that meaning on the offer,' Sir George remarked, 'and really it was very good-natured on Disraeli's part. It was so, all the more, when I remembered our contest over the affair of the Kaffir chiefs and their allowance. You see, I rather had the best of that, and his friends chaffed him about it.' Sir George was his own political party all through life, so far as he was a politician at all. Disraeli asked no pledges, but, as Sir George observed, 'We were far divided in our views, and I should have been in revolt almost before I had taken my seat. Therefore I declined with thanks.'

Meanwhile, being free of official shackles, he hurled himself against the movement, rampant in England, to throw off the Colonies. He was Pro-Consul at large, under warrant of a duty for which he held himself accountable to the English-speaking people. He doubted whether he was not, thus, doing even better work, than he would have found to his hand as an employed Governor. There rang from end to end of the country a shriek of dismemberment : 'Cut the painter, chop off the Colonies, they are a burden to us; we should confine ourselves to ourselves !'

'It is difficult,' said Sir George, 'to make anybody, who was not in that struggle, understand it. One would have called it simply freakish, if the possible outcome had been less grave. It was a strange fit to seize upon the country, and unfortunately it expressed the view of nearly all the leading statesmen. Cut the painter ! You cannot imagine any sensible person of these later, and regenerate, days having such an idea. Throw away Australasia or South Africa ! You have heard my retort on such a demand. Who had the right, to tell another man, of the same blood, that he was no longer a Briton, because he lived many sea miles distant ? Who could answer that ? None ! It was all a whimsy, a craze, a nightmare, which will never return—Never, Never !'

Sir George instructed the country, by word and pen, on the true value and destiny of the Colonies. He moved about, a crusader, indignant at separatism, eloquent to knot, and re-knot, the painter. For the slash of the knife he offered federation, and, springing therefrom, a happier, better world altogether. He did not doubt, to his last days, that the peril of the

Empire was very real. Neither did he doubt that it was overcome, largely by the wisdom and foresight of the Queen. 'But for her action,' he declared in so many words, 'events would most probably have ended in the cutting adrift of some of the colonies. She saw true, and clear, and far, as the Prince Consort when alive had seen, and the Anglo-Saxon race has reason to be thankful.'

Wherever he had been, Sir George Grey had endeavoured, in his own phrase, to extend the liberties and rights of the people. 'Thus,' he instanced, 'until I went to the Cape, no judge had been appointed to the supreme court there, except from England. On vacancies occurring, I named two local men, both, I fancy, of Dutch family, thus breaking down a bad custom. I felt that it was impossible to govern a nation upon terms which hurt its manhood and dignity.' His crusade in England was on a like note, and eventually it found him a parliamentary candidate for Newark.

'Immediately my friends heard of the vacancy,' he narrated, 'they proposed that I should stand for it. I did so, an independent Liberal, and I was ostracised by the party leaders, who had another candidate they wanted to get in. I suppose I was too advanced altogether, and indeed I preached a kind of new gospel. It included emigration; a handmaid to federation when the Colonies had ripened. Then I was for free education, and disestablishment all round, as a necessary thing in relation to Christianity—in fact as one of its main doctrines.

THE ROMANCE OF A PRO-CONSUL

Farther, I advocated Irish Home Rule, even drafting a short Bill, and in fine I was for a variety of innovations.'.

Apart from all else, he understood that his Liberal rival was required in the House of Commons, to help Cardwell with military affairs. Anyhow, he gathered that impression from a visit which Mr. A. J. Mundella, journeying over from Nottingham, paid him at Newark. The encounter supplied a good story, and its manner was Sir George Grey in a characteristic mood. This was how he gravely met Mr. Mundella's gentle overture, ' Now, won't you withdraw from the contest ? '—

' Yes, I quite see the difficulty. You want somebody to assist Cardwell. However well your suggestion might obviate the difficulty, I have an alternative which I think would equally suit. I had a military training, I did very creditably as a student at Sandhurst, I served with the colours, and I attained the rank of captain. I shall be glad to show you my papers, proving my knowledge of military affairs ; and altogether, if your War Minister requires somebody to prompt him, I don't see why I should not fill the place as satisfactorily as another.'

' Oh,' exclaimed Mr. Mundella, ' there's no use in coming to you with anything, for you always make a joke of it.' So they parted, and laughing, over the years, at the incident, Sir George said : ' You know Mundella was a capital fellow, of sterling ability and many qualities, but I'm afraid he was never a humorist.'

Sir George was not to be member for Newark, since, in the long run, to save the loss of a Liberal seat, he retired. His committee put it to him that this was the rule of the road, and he felt it no sacrifice to quit the field. The tribes had to be pacified, but how different the methods in primitive and civilised society!

Two tribes fell out during his first Governorship of New Zealand, and they must settle their difference by combat. Sir George deprecated such things, as not being conducive to the welfare of the Colony. No sooner did he hear of the duel, than he ordered a warship to up-steam and carry him to the spot. He was put ashore, when the day was breaking, at a point still sixteen miles from the combatants. He obtained a horse for himself, another for an orderly, and the pair were given rein.

'I believe,' he told, 'that our first mounts proved not very good, only, at a farm on the way, we were able to replace them with better. Our ride was across rough country, innocent of roads, but we reached our destination just as the campaign opened for the day. I waited a minute to master the state of parties, then galloped straight between them, and called out "Stop! Stop!" Amazed at my appearance, they just shouted along their ranks "Te Kuwana"—the Maori effort to say "The Governor."

'As I had ridden into the fusilade, a chief was shot in the neck, with the penalty that he could never afterwards turn his head. Happily he was not looking over his shoulder at the moment, for that would have been an awkward position in which to be left. My plunge into the battle was a little risky, but I calculated that the Maoris would, most likely, be glad of an excuse to stop fighting. Combatants who fall out easily, generally are. They regard as a benefactor, anybody who can rescue them from their scrape, with due form of ceremony and guarantee of dignity. My order to the Maoris, desiring peace, was obeyed.'

This is the Sir George Grey whose doings you follow with the keenest tingle of interest—Grey, Pro-Consul. But his other activities all grouped round this signature, and they are to be read with it. From England he went back to New Zealand, thinking he could best influence the Old World from the shores of the New World. He sat himself down in the remote solitude of Kawau, among his books, and every morning his heart beat round the Empire, a morning drum.

Twice Governor of New Zealand, he was yet to be its Prime Minister, a record which is unique. Being asked to work in New Zealand domestic politics, he replied : 'I will be a messenger if in that capacity I can usefully serve the State.' Yet, once more, you turn to the romance maker and discover him taking down, by the lake side of Rotorua, that of Hine-Moa. He rescued it, a Hero and Leander legend, with a variation, from the Maori ages, and placed it, a pearl, among his other delvings from Polynesian mythology. The story captured him, with its naïve charm, when first he heard it from the lips of a chief, and many should know it.

''Tis odd,' he made the comment, ' how frequently like incidents occur in the mythology of diverse races. By what means were they communicated ? As I have pointed out, in my compilation of Maori legends, there is one of Maui, which recalls to you the finding of Arthur, in Tennyson's " Idylls of the King." The same legendary idea occurs ; a child cradled by the sea, none knowing that it had any other parent.'

' Now, O Governor,' spoke the Maori chief, ' look round you and listen to me, for there is something worth seeing here.' Sir George was sitting on the very spot where sat Hine-Moa, the great ancestress of the tribe, when she swam the lake to join her sweetheart Tutanekai. She was a maiden of rare beauty and high rank, and many young men desired to wed her. She found escape from these perplexities in a long swim to her choice, Tutanekai. But the Maori chief goes forward with the idyll, and must be followed word for word, as Sir George wrote :—

. . . .

At the place where she landed there is a hot spring, separated from the lake only by a narrow ledge of rocks. Hine-Moa got into this to warm herself, for she was trembling all over, partly from the cold, after swimming in the night across the wide lake of Rotorua, and partly also, perhaps, from modesty at the thought of meeting Tutanekai.

Whilst the maiden was thus warming herself in

the hot spring, Tutanekai happened to feel thirsty and said to his servant, 'Bring me a little water.' So his servant went to fetch water for him, and drew it from the lake in a calabash, close to the spot where Hine-Moa was sitting.

The maiden, who was frightened, called out to him in a gruff voice like that of a man : 'Whom is that water for ?'

He replied, ' It's for Tutanekai.'

'Give it here, then,' said Hine-Moa. And he gave her the water and she drank, and, having finished drinking, she purposely threw down the calabash and broke it.

Then the servant asked her, 'What business had you to break the calabash of Tutanekai ?' but Hine-Moa did not say a word in answer.

The servant then went back, and Tutanekai said to him, ' Where is the water I told you to bring me ?'

So he answered, ' Your calabash was broken.'

And his master asked him, 'Who broke it ?' And he answered, ' The man who is in the bath.'

And Tutanekai said to him, 'Go back again, then, and fetch me some water.'

He therefore took a second calabash and went back and drew water in the calabash from the lake; and Hine-Moa again said to him, ' Whom is that water for ?'

So the slave answered as before, 'For Tutanekai.'

And the maiden again said, 'Give it to me, for I am thirsty.' And the slave gave it to her and she drank and purposely threw down the calabash and broke it.

And these occurrences took place repeatedly, between those two persons.

At last the slave went again to Tutanekai, who said to him, 'Where is the water for me ?'

And his servant answered, 'It is all gone ; your calabashes have been broken.'

'By whom ?' said his master.

'Didn't I tell you that there is a man in the bath ?' answered the servant.

'Who is the fellow ?' said Tutanekai.

'How can I tell ?' replied the slave. 'Why, he's a stranger.'

'Didn't he know the water was for me ?' said Tutanekai. 'How did the rascal dare to break my calabashes ! Why, I shall die from rage !'

Then Tutanekai threw on some clothes and caught hold of his club, and away he went and came to the bath and called out 'Where's that fellow who broke my calabashes ?'

And Hine-Moa knew the voice, that the sound of it was that of the beloved of her heart ; and she hid herself under the overhanging rocks of the hot spring. But her hiding was hardly a real hiding ; rather a bashful concealing of herself from Tutanekai that he might not find her at once, only after trouble and careful search for her.

So he went feeling about, along the banks of the hot spring, searching everywhere, whilst she lay coyly hid under the ledges of the rocks, peeping out, wondering when she should be found.

At last he caught hold of a hand and cried out, ' Hullo, who's this ? '

And Hine-Moa answered : 'It's I, Tutanekai.'

And he said : 'But who are you ? Who's I ? '

Then she spoke louder, and said : 'It's I, 'tis Hine-Moa.'

And he said : ' Ho ! ho ! ho ! Can such in very truth be the case ? Let us two, then, go to my house.'

And she answered ' Yes.'

And she rose up in the water as beautiful as the wild white hawk, and stepped upon the edge of the bath as graceful as the shy white crane. And he threw garments over her, and took her, and they proceeded to his house and reposed there, and thenceforth, according to the ancient laws of the Maoris, they were man and wife.

XVIII

A FATHER OF FEDERATION

Mr. Gladstone and Sir George Grey ploughed different seas, under charter from the English-speaking race. One flew his pennant in the nearer waters, the other in the farther. Now and then they met, but briefly, as ships do which pass in the night.

'What I saw of Mr. Gladstone,' said Sir George, ' was mostly at official gatherings, or gatherings arising out of official life. One session, however, during which I was in England, we dined almost every Wednesday evening at the same London house.

'Mr. Gladstone was always a most charming personality, and I recall his friendliness in walking up with me to the hall of ceremonies, when I received the honorary degree at Cambridge. He also was to have the honour conferred upon him that day, and it was considerate on his part to convoy me along, as I knew few people at Cambridge, the result of absence from England.

'As to public affairs, I suspect that he and I held widely different views, at all events on some subjects. Like everybody else, I recognised in him a command-

195   o 2

ing figure, but I am bound to say that his greatness seemed to me to lie in carrying out ideas, after they had been suggested by others, rather than in working them out himself.'

Sir George meant that Mr. Gladstone's genius as a statesman, was constructive more than creative, the fashioner of progress. For himself, a solitary idea sufficed to keep his heart warm, even in the colds of age—the federation of the English-speaking people. In one of the last letters he received from David Livingstone, there was the request, 'Write me often because you cheer me up.' It was always possible to cheer Sir George up on federation; that set him aglow.

There were few to listen when he first preached the federal idea ; he cried in the wilderness, but he did not cease to cry. He waited long for the echoes to come back, and they did come, with interest, too, when negotiations for an Anglo-American treaty of arbitration went afoot. Then, the negotiations tumbled through, whereat he said : ' Oh, the road may be a gradual one, with hills and stops, but there it lies, traced by destiny, and in the fulness of time it will be trodden.'

Peering into the twentieth century, one who would never see it, he foretold that its great problem would be this of Anglo-Saxon federation. It was not for us to dip into the future, farther than we could reasonably behold, but so far we were not only entitled, but bound, to go. He doubted whether any question, equal in importance to federation, had ever before engaged the attention of so large a portion of mankind. On' that account he put forward with diffidence, the views which, after much reflection, he had formed upon it.

By Anglo-Saxon federation, he understood joint action, in the interests of mankind, on the part of those owning allegiance to the English tongue. Forms and methods might take care of themselves, so the thing itself was begotten. Yet that could only be, if the ties sought to be woven were elastic, free and freedom-giving. He wanted a golden chain, binding men to men the Anglo-Saxon world over, but a curb · chain nowhere.

' I am,' he spoke, ' merely expressing what is gene-rally agreed, when I say that the end of the nineteenth century has brought us to a critical period in the history of the world. Systems of government do not last for ever ; they decay and have to be replaced. The most perfect of machines wears itself out, and another has to be substituted.

' Not merely that, but the new one has to be of a different design, adapted to a fresh, most likely a severer, set of circumstances. A man who refused to utilise the wisdom and resources of his age in machinery, would be regarded as a madman. It is the same in the economy of the human family ; to dread wise and ordered change is to court trouble.'

Thus, Sir George reasoned that we had arrived at an epoch of federation, the application of which would be something new, only the conditions needing it had not arisen before. The ancients had not discovered the art of securing political representation, or, what the moderns called the principle of federation. It was not necessary for the ancients, as it had become for the moderns. Simply, the conditions of the world had changed, and that on two planes.

In the past, there had been the continual discovery and peopling of new countries. No more remained to be discovered ; no corner of the globe remained unknown to us. We knew what each nation was engaged in doing, and we were able to estimate, with some measure of assurance, what it would continue doing. Next, the mass of the people had gained a potent voice in the management of affairs. Democracy was coming to the throne, if it had not quite grasped all the trappings.

The key of what was to be, rested in those two facts, which made the world so different a working-machine from what it had been. And the using of the key was primarily confided to the Anglo-Saxon race, since it occupied the greatest extent of the globe, and included what was ripest and best in democracy.

'Everywhere,' Sir George showed, 'our people are working, with might and main, to develop the resources of the earth. They are characterised by a common language, a common literature, and common laws. Shakespeare, Milton, the riches of our classic literature, belong as much to these new nations over-sea, as they do to the Mother Country. The men and women of Anglo-Saxon stock carry with them, wherever they go, the one faith of Christianity.

'Really, there could not be anything but a unity, a oneness, in the whole structure upon which the race rests. If the progress, in natural federation, has been so great, through years when South Africa, or New Zealand, was far distant from England, when there were no swift steamers and no cables under the sea, what must it now become? Such wonderful changes has modern science brought about, that the peoples of Greater Britain and America are next-door neighbours to the folks in the Old Country.

'Nay, daily and hourly counsel goes on between all parts of the world, bringing the wisdom of the whole to each point. Communities, separated by seas and continents, are able to discuss with each other, on the minute, what action is for the highest interests of all. It is impossible that the federation we see existing in the incessant congress of the civilised world, can ever be gone back upon.'

A pretty incident of Sir George Grey's tour through Australia as a tribune might have been reported in London next morning. This was following the first conference, held in Sydney, on the great subject of Australasian federation. Sir George, after a season of heather burning, was taking ship at Sydney, to return to New Zealand. A multitude of people streamed forth to bid him good-bye, and he walked down their ranks to the steamer.

'As I was stepping on board,' he told the episode,

'I noticed a lad smoking a cigarette. Being near him, I remarked quietly, "What a pity it is to see a bright boy like you smoking ! You are very young to smoke. I am sure if you consider the expense it will lead you into, and perhaps the injury to your health, you will not smoke."

'He looked up at me for a minute as if thinking, and then, with the declaration, "I'll never smoke again," threw the cigarette from him. By this time the crowd had noted what was transpiring, and they cheered the lad again and again, much, I'm afraid, to his confusion. Now, wasn't that a nice thing for a boy to do ? It pleased me wonderfully.'

The proofs of federation by cable, which Sir George selected, were not, however, related to himself. One was the auspicious and happy event of the birth of a child, in direct succession to the English throne, Prince Edward of York. 'Why,' he paused, 'that was known within an hour on the farthest shores of Greater Britain, and the news, I can assure you, received with as keen a joy as in England.' The second case was the historic London dock strike, of which he said, 'Not merely was that struggle followed from hour to hour in Australasia, but encouragements and assistance from Australasian workers to their comrades at home, swept continually across the seas.'

There was already union between the different branches of the Anglo-Saxon family, and all we had to do was to afford it assistance in growing and forming. Ever, we must provide more adequate

means for utilising the onward tide of humanity,
striving after higher ideals. We needed to have life
permeated with all the helps and lights that were
possible ; not to shut these out as they became
available.

There had been disturbances to the growth of
Anglo-Saxon union, and opportunities for its further-
ance had been thrown away. Perhaps the greatest
disturbance was the war between the Northern and
Southern States of America. 'It arose,' Sir George
noted, 'out of the one great flaw in that wonderful
creation, the American Constitution. Strangely enough,
the Constitution omitted to make any provision for
dealing with slavery, and inevitably, in course of time,
came dispute and war.' Yet, the strands of race held
unbroken through that trial, and the future was
secure.

Sir George Grey found himself reinforced, in so
believing, by the opinion of General Grant. This
he heard from Sir T. Fowell Buxton, who had
travelled in America with Mr. W. E. Forster, while
Grant was President. The General took his English
visitors for a drive, and his talk was of military
matters and his horses, until they were nearly back at
Washington. Suddenly, he went off on the subject
of an alliance between Great Britain and the United
States, his hopes and expectations of it. He added
that he should not live to witness the drawing together,
but he was certain it must become a great power in
the world, especially on sea.

'Well,' Sir George commented, 'if General Grant, a man of singularly practical character, was among the prophets, I am quite content to be in his company.'

When he talked of the federation of the British Empire, or of the larger welding in which he had belief, Sir George would declare, 'No good service is rendered by creating difficulties ahead. We may be certain of this—that each generation, as it comes rolling on, will hold its own views upon every subject, differing widely, perhaps, from the views of its predecessors. The essential thing, in all government, is to secure to the people at large, the power of enacting the laws they deem to be the wisest and best suited to the circumstances of their age.'

Thus, while he had worked out definite lines of federation, he was content if principles were accepted. 'No man,' he argued, 'should presume to lay down the law in such a matter; just let the vision be realised by natural process. Be there the hewing of materials, and the building would follow by and by. If it were possible to solidify the English-speaking people for common purposes, the gain to them, and to mankind, would be splendid. The blessings of federation were a hundredfold.

'Why,' said Sir George, 'war would practically die off the face of the earth. The armed camp which burdens the Old World, enslaves the nations, and impedes progress, would disappear. The Anglo-Saxon race, going together, could determine the balance of power for a fully peopled earth. Such a moral force would be irresistible, and debate would take the place of war, in the settlement of international disputes. If the arbitrament of reason, ousts the arbitrament of war, a new and beautiful world is unveiled.'

It was because Sir George saw, in federation, a vista of brighter life for the masses, that he was so persuaded an advocate of it, so keen a believer in its realisation. As a result of the cohesion of the race, we should have all life quickened and developed; unemployed energies called into action in many places where they lay stagnant. Below federation, the very essence of it, was decentralisation, the getting of the people fairly spread over the earth, not huddled into a few places where decay would follow overcrowding.

'Every section of the British Empire,' Sir George detailed this point, 'having complete self-government would contain its own life within itself, would offer the highest opportunities to the labours of its citizens. Whenever you constitute a new centre of authority you create a basis of general activity, which, in its turn, has off-shoots. There would be more employment; the waste lands of the Old World, and the still untilled ones of the New World, would be taken up. Federation is not the mere grouping of us together, but the settlement of problems that have long been forcing themselves to the front. Difficulties which we can ill solve now, which appear to block our path, we should be able to settle with ease.'

Sir George discerned an element, not fully dreamt of, which would immensely strengthen the federal idea. It was the influence of women, growing to be a powerful factor in the affairs of the world. This sweet authority would tend to keep nations from plunging into scenes of bloodshed. It would be a blessed assistance towards the peace of the world in times of excitement, and so a bulwark for federation, which was the creator of peace.

Finally, the rise of the Anglo-Saxon, by means of federation, would benefit the world in respect to religion and language — kernels of all advancement. It would mean the triumph of what, if carried out, was the highest moral system that man in all his history had known — Christianity. And it would imply the dominance of probably the richest language that ever existed, our own English.

So speaking, Sir George Grey summed up : 'Given a universal code of morals and a universal tongue, how far would be the step to that last great federation, the brotherhood of mankind, which Tennyson and Burns have sung to us ? '

* *Those who desire to study Sir George Grey's full and final scheme for Anglo-Saxon federation, may refer to the ' Contemporary Review' of August* 1894, *where it appeared as an article by the present writer.*

XIX

WAITING TO GO

'I AM just waiting my time to go, meanwhile doing what little I can that may be useful to my fellow-men.'

These were the words of Sir George Grey, and none could better express the closing years of his life. If he might sow, in some wayside garden, an idea for the common happiness, he counted that a day on the active list. It made him feel young again, blowing the old fires red and rosy. Ever, he held to his tryst with Dean Stanley.

'One evening,' it had been made, 'the Dean and myself were walking round Westminster Abbey, as the doors were being closed. It was during my visit to England, after my last Governorship, and the Dean was full of the restorations then being carried out on the Chapter House. Naturally, I had the keenest interest in whatever affected the ancient seat of the House of Commons, regarding it as a shrine of constitutional government.

'Dean Stanley wanted to show me everything, to explain the whole place. He told me of a theory of his that the Commons, while sitting there in a circular room, probably had no parties, so called. They were grouped in a ring, not confronting each other sharply, antagonistically, and everything went on with quietness. But when they moved across to St. Stephen's, they found themselves set opposite-wise, which fact may have tended to create the party system. That was the idea put to me by the Dean, though how far he applied it, I do not recollect.

'Anyhow, he was anxious that I should study the Chapter House under him, but it was too late to do it that evening. "Never mind," he said, "let us wait until things are more complete and we shall go in together." "Oh," I answered, "I really need not trouble you. I can look in myself one afternoon." "No, no," he insisted, with much good nature, "I want to be your guide. You must promise that you will not go there without me." "Very well then," I assured him, "I shall wait until you take me."

'The Dean and myself did not, as it happened, meet again at that period, nor were we, by the decree of Providence, ever to meet. Thus, I shall not see the earliest home of the House of Commons, as it has been restored, for I promised.'

There swam in Sir George's recollection, a little story touching the evolution of the body politic, during his own time. It was like Maūi of Maori legend, and Arthur 'by wild Dundagil on the Cornish sea,' in that he scarce knew whence it came. He inclined to link it, a whiff of airy gossip, with two of the most strenuous middle Victorians, but would hold no names certain.

'At all events,' he said, 'the Cabinet was formerly a smaller body than it now is, and less formal in its proceedings. The members would drop in, with the newspapers in their hands, and take a chair, here or there, as the case might be. A quite large Cabinet being created, the Prime Minister suggested, "Gentlemen, had we not better sit round the table?" The suggestion met with approval, and the Premier made to take his place at the head of the table. Thereupon, a colleague caught up a chair, put it beside that of the Premier, and sat down with the remark, "There is no such thing as a President of the Cabinet."'

For a good while, Sir George Grey spoke of himself as being in England, only to bid England farewell. Some fine morning he would pack his trunks, and sail south to those who knew him best. Every step in New Zealand was a greeting; in London a mile was bare. Once he did pack his trunks, but the fine morning never arrived.

When rallied about that, Sir George defended himself, 'I suppose I want to see what I can do, as one of your most eminent statesmen did, in his youth. He went to a small island, then connected with the family property, and studied laboriously for a whole winter. He desired to establish what was in him, what exertion he was likely to be equal to, in the world's affairs. Then, lest trouble should ever befall him, he, another time, went into lodgings to test how little it was really possible to live upon. I don't recall at what figure the experiment worked out, but it was a ridiculously small one.'

A spirit, kindred in its attitude to the seriousness of life, animated Sir George Grey, even as he spoke. Affairs in England seemed critical, and he would stay on to watch them, since any hint might be of import. In London there beat the heart of the Empire, and he would keep his ear to it. He heard most clearly through that trumpet, the endless roll of London's traffic. Moreover, the great city, while she hardly nodded to Sir George, smote him afresh with the spell which is hers alone. Oh to be in London !

So dates moved past, and Sir George Grey, as he waned under the growing load, realised that he and Greater Britain would be no more together. That thought he parried, not liking to admit it, but the painter was cut when he resigned his place in the Parliament of New Zealand. It had to be done, therefore let it be done ; but it was a shock, like losing a limb to the surgeon.

A hail from Greater Britain became thrice welcome, and that of Mahomed Naser Eben took Sir George by siege, especially its quaintness and literary touch. When Governor of the Cape Colony, he sent word up-country, by David Livingstone, that he would be glad of any manuscripts throwing light upon the Greeks and Romans in Africa. To a British man-of-war, making patrol of the Mombasa coast, there rowed out a boat, having a respectable old Arab gentleman in the stern-sheets. He handed up a parcel, desiring it to be delivered to Sir George Grey at Cape Town. Sir George had left South Africa for New Zealand, and the manuscripts, as the contents of the bundle proved, were sent after him.

'But nobody could read them,' he stated, 'until here, as I learn, an Assyrian gentleman has been visiting Auckland. What is my surprise, on opening this envelope, to find everything made clear in English. including Mahomed Naser Eben's letter to me. He addresses me as a cavern of hospitality, which is very handsome, and a phrase with a true Oriental flavour. Unluckily, he appears to have got lost for two years in that part of Africa marked Oman on the map. Hence a delay with him, in sending the manuscripts, but he need not have apologised, my single feeling being gladness that he discovered himself again.'

It was nigh forty years since Mahomed Naser Eben wrote, and in the interval many skies had changed. Two had been apart, a sundered heaven, the doing of that tragedy which ever lies in wait upon romance. But they came together, as the clouds were gathering, and upon them the sun ray of Mahomed Naser Eben could sparkle. Sir George had scarce mastered the mystery of his epistle when he was drawing out a reply to it. His only doubt was whether the erudite Arab might not have changed his address !

'We are about the same age,' Rewi imparted to Sir George Grey in New Zealand, 'and when I go, your time will be approaching.' Sir George recalled this, on hearing that Rewi had been gathered to his Maori fathers. He was buried in a grave which 'The Governor' had selected, near the spot where the last fight took place between the Maoris and the English. 'We should lie together,' Rewi also held, 'as being the two people who brought peace to New Zealand.' Sir George's voice shook when telling this proof of Maori affection, as his eyes turned dim at reading an address sent him, to fabled London, by the men of that race in the Cook Islands.

'Our word to you, O Grey,' they saluted him, 'is this. We wish you happiness and health, and to know that our love goes forth with this letter. We wish to tell you that your name will never be forgotten by the Maori people in these islands. Many of us knew you in New Zealand, but all have heard of the great things done by you, for European and for Maori, in that country. May God's blessing rest upon you, and give peace and happiness to you, who have done so much for the peace and happiness of others, in your long and honoured life.'

An illness brought that life very near the ebb, and friends wondered, of an evening, if next morning they would hear his simple, tender, 'Good-bye to you.' Sir George waited ready, abiding in the faith, witnessing of it, 'Man should have religion as his guide in all things. I feel that God communicates with His creatures when they please. He lets them know what is right and wrong, even argues with them.

'It was a comfort to me, in trying hours, to feel that I was working according to the way of my Maker, so far as I could comprehend it. Perhaps I most experienced this nearness of an all-wise Providence while I was amid the heathen acres of the far south. You seemed to be communing with the Great Spirit more intimately in these lonely haunts than elsewhere. I have always been supported by the belief in God's goodness, as manifested to me. My judgment is that man cannot prosper if he falls from faith, by which I mean trust in a Supreme Being.'

There were no shadows, no terrors for Sir George Grey, in what we chilly term death. He could look blithely along the road, ready to greet it with outstretched hand when it turned the corner. Just, he waited to go, as he might have waited for a sure arm on which to lean. He saw the lamps afar.

' When one has reached an old age,' was his vista, ' the thought of death should not be a sad thought. It is not sad with me, but on the contrary pleasant, meaning a happy event to be welcomed. Death ! I do not believe in death, except that the flesh dies ; for the spirit goes on and on. Terror of death is necessary, in order to keep men and animals from killing themselves. That is all.

' The future is mystery, for none have returned to inform us what is there. But our knowledge of the Creator teaches us that His goodness will be greater and greater towards His creatures. If the babe leaves the womb, to come into such a beautiful world as ours, how beautiful a world may we not pass into ? It was terrible to the babe to be torn from the womb, but it had no idea what loving hands were waiting for it.

'We have God's assurance that He is always good to His creatures who die, and we may be satisfied. Really, there is a lovely romance in death, in the spirit being released from the clay, which, through ill-health or old age, has grown to burden it. That spirit, struggling onward and upward, shakes itself free and soars off, bright, fresh, eternal, to the other world for which it had been preparing. It purifies itself, by throwing aside a weight, and thus death is not death but life ; another birth, life in death.'

Not then, not for another year and more, was the departure to be. 'Put my watch under my pillow,' he looked up cheerily to those at his bedside ; 'and thank you for taking care of it while I have been ill. It's the watch the Queen gave me, and I like to have it near.' But that illness sapped and mined him, even while he proposed, 'Oh, yes, we'll go down to Chelsea and inspect Carlyle's old house. I'll try and fill it again with him, in particular the room at the top which he built to be noise-proof, and which wasn't.' The visit was never paid, but the celebration of the Queen's reign of sixty years still found Sir George able to be about.

That was right well, for how many had made such a contribution to the history and dominion of the reign ? Truly, dreams had come about, since he listened to the bells of Plymouth, when taking passage by the *Beagle*. Here was goodly proof of things achieved for the happiness of men, such as even he had scarce dared to imagine. The fairies had been working.

Sir George followed, in imagination, the nations of the realm as they walked through London, its capital, while all the world wondered. He attended, in heart, the simple service at St. Paul's Cathedral, where he himself was to find a last resting-place, sleeping with the worthies. He could picture the great fleet, seal of the sea-power which made all possible, spread itself athwart the Solent. Yes, Sir George Grey heard, from afar, the 'tumult and the shouting,' and they rounded off his own career as the True Briton and True Imperialist.

He heard also, amid the glorious rumble, of another royal progress made by the Queen. It was at her Highland home, the spectators the eternal hills which lie about it. For caparisoning there was a donkey-chaise, and for escort a Highlander, carrying the shawls. The Queen was bound for the manse, across the fields by the river-side, to pray with the minister's wife that he, being ill, might be made whole.

That was the royal progress Sir George Grey would best have liked to see, because it held the key to the other. From it, he sent, by his friend the Prime Minister of New Zealand, a last message to

Greater Britain. 'Give the people of New Zealand my love,' it ran, 'and may God have you in His keeping.' It was the closing of the book, save for the blank pages which occur at the end.

'It's all light,' was Selwyn's dying exclamation in Maori. None knew the Maori words that Sir George Grey murmured, and none doubted what they were. To us, the island race of two worlds,

> Under the Cross of Gold,
> That shines over city and river,
> There he shall rest for ever,
> Among the wise and the bold.

PRINTED BY
SPOTTISWOODE AND CO., NEW-STREET SQUARE
LONDON

www.ingramcontent.com/pod-product-compliance
Lightning Source LLC
Chambersburg PA
CBHW030117030726
47498CB00007B/2428